Dark Knights, Crystal Daze

Dark Knights, Crystal Daze

The third novel in the **DEADLY DIAMONDS** Trilogy

CHYNA DIXON-KENNEDY

Dark Knights, Crystal Daze
The third novel in the Deadly Diamonds Trilogy

iUniverse books may be ordered through booksellers or by contacting:

iUniverse
1663 Liberty Drive
Bloomington, IN 47403
www.iuniverse.com
1-800-Authors (1-800-288-4677)

ISBN: 978-1-4917-6977-5 (sc)
ISBN: 978-1-4917-6976-8 (e)

Print information available on the last page.

iUniverse rev. date: 06/29/2015

ACKNOWLEDGMENTS

Thank you to Almighty God for your
divine strength & support.

Andrea Adonis and Ryan Delp- Thanks for your
level of professionalism in delivering this book.

For future releases, follow the author at
www.facebook.com/chyna.dixonkennedy

Email inquiries to: **cdkbooks@gmail.com**

Please look for these additional titles in the
DEADLY DIAMONDS Trilogy:

Ice Palace, Crystal Dreams

Crystal Ice, Cold-Blooded

Crystal Clear, Rock Star Revealed!

New! Self-help guide by Chyna Dixon-Kennedy...

Hollywood Glam: Recipes 4 Living the Celebrity Life

This book is dedicated to all of the readers
out there… my fans fuel my passion!

One that was cut short, mostly due to the presence of too many secrets! But it didn't matter now, for Crystal had already identified who this particular secret was specifically pertaining to. She already knew the greasy character that was involved in this sorrowful tragedy.

Scanning the bloody handwriting that was sloppily left on the cement block wall, Crystal got the message loud and clear:

"Betrayal is a Beast"

What's done in the dark, must come to the light; and in time all things are revealed. Someday, she would find a way to make that man pay. Pay mightily for snuffing out the life of *one of her dearest friends...*

CHAPTER 1

Every hero has a dark patch that stains the past. It overshadows the glory, taints the righteousness, and besmirches an otherwise spotless reputation. In the annals of time, it reeks of foulness, and leaves a malodorous mark upon one's memory. It stinks of shame, bitter remorse, regret, and humiliation. It tragically spoils one's future eligibility for 'sainthood.' However, it does not have to be an irrevocable state.

Once that hero learns how to control personal behavior and overcome all adversity, he (or she) can reign triumphant in the end. Then people can simply choose to remember the legacy, not the lingering stench of rotting leftovers. Throughout history many human beings have been found guilty, at one point or another, of committing acts that were considered sinful, vulgar, obscene, lewd, profane, coarse, indecent, filthy, or downright wicked. It could've either been through thoughtless childhood pranks, the follies of youth, or deplorable lifestyle choices forged during young adulthood. The excesses of life can lead one down a slippery slope of evil, debauchery, depravity, and repeated sessions of incredibly bad decision-making.

Yet, all is not lost…

It's never too late to turn it all around, and *finish up strong*! This was the hopeful dream that Dr. Crystal Knight-Davenport clung to right now, as she drifted randomly in and out of consciousness. A familiar voice kept pulling her back to this realm, but she was already existing in a parallel universe somewhere over yonder. She kept on vacillating between two worlds.

As she floated back to random scenes from her childhood years, she realized that she was merely an anachronistic specimen that didn't quite fit in with this particular setting. She was now a strange visitor from another time period. Yet she felt warm, well fed, and surrounded by a gaggle of other adolescents. She wanted to stay and hang out with them a little longer, but was becoming distinctly aware of a shrill beeping noise that kept invading her fading reminiscences.

There it was again: a combination of sounds, like a baritone male voice mixed with some annoying bells.

Chiming bells. Rhyming bells. Ringing bells. Jingling bells. Bells…bells…bells! If only she could just get up and turn down the volume on the radio. Or shut the maddening repetitions off altogether. Her brain sent a message to her legs to start moving, but nothing happened. She tried to will herself to become mobile, but instead just laid there motionless. The more she attempted to command her uncooperative body parts, the more frustrating the whole situation became. She couldn't even yell out for assistance. The words came to her dry, parched lips- with nothing but air escaping.

As her form began to twitch with agitation, she felt a slight needle prick somewhere on her being. Suddenly a rush of warm liquids entered her veins and those feelings of euphoria began to wash over her once more in waves. Slowly she sank into that nirvana known as nostalgia; remembering events from the happier days.

Now she was back around Christmas time with her teenage buddies. If only she could truly go back to that era. If only she could start all over again and do things differently. If only she could change some of the choices that she made along the way in life. If only she could rewrite history. *If only...*

Crystal knew that she couldn't travel back through time, yet here she was re-living the past. Doomed to make the same mistakes over and over again, she yearned to have a different outcome. She hoped that it was not too late. She was finally ready to face the hard truth about herself. She was ready to embrace her weaknesses and learn the essential lessons that needed to be inculcated into her spirit. God was dealing with her in some sort of way; and as her soul hung in the very balance between life and death, she prayed that she could come out of this trip on the side of victory.

Little did Crystal know that her existence was about to transcend to the next level. Little did she know that all of her pain and suffering was not for naught. Although she had nearly paid the ultimate price, one final sacrifice would need to be made to complete the prophesy. Before she could reap the bountiful harvest that awaited her, she had to sow a seed. But hadn't she already given enough? What more could God possibly want her to release, before she could truly savor the sweet taste of peace in her life? And how could she ever have closure, without a serious sense of fairness?

Coming full circle just prior to her fortieth birthday, she realized that the dramatic conclusion to this story was still as yet unwritten. Thus, there was still a chance to *make it right*. With enough strength, courage, and forgiveness- there was an opportunity to enjoy God's love, grace and limitless mercy in her life.

If only she could rise to the occasion. If only she weren't running out of time. If only she could bring her conscience to be in alignment with His divine will forever. If only she could get up from this physical position, and leave the confines of this mental prison.

As the powerful sedative coursed through her arteries, she slipped into a montage of flashback memories. Vowing to hold on a little longer, while fighting 'til the very end, Crystal made up her mind that this was not it. She did not want to go into the light. No, not just yet! There was still some unfinished business that warranted her attention first. Things still needed to be done. Her agenda must be completed, before she could have everlasting Redemption to wipe her slate clean.

Before she sang her final swan song, exiting this realm forever, there was just one thing that she needed to receive: *Revenge*. For she would never rest in eternity before she had it. She had promised to move Heaven and Earth to seek a sense of righteousness and justice.

Just when the tides were beginning to shift in her favor, she nearly got herself killed. Now she would have to emerge from this pit of darkness, a black abyss that banished her to oblivion. Like a phoenix rising from the ashes, she would get up from this place of despair to soar high amongst the heavens once more.

She had just enough fight left in her body to successfully accomplish this mission. Failure was not an option this time. If she had to give every last cell of her being to exact sweet revenge, then let it be so done.

After all, she did know a little something about avenging an untimely death. Now it was time to seek retribution for the murder of her beautiful older sister, Kim. Thirty-five years was not long enough to fully erase the pain, so Crystal kept on chanting to herself:

Sangre por sangre. Sangre por sangre.

Blood for blood! Blood for blood!

It was time to hunt down a sadistic serial killer, a demented child destroyer. One way or another, Crystal would find the head vampire of that evil cult, Mr. Juan Rosario Ortega. The only way to stop the killing of the innocents, and the suffering of countless survivors, was to cut the head of the serpent completely off. Therefore she valiantly sought to bring his contemptible life *to an abrupt end…*

CHAPTER 2

Detective Dellevega nervously glanced at his Rolex, watching the hired nurse administer that last injection. Glad that he was granted a leave of absence from his stressful job, he wondered obliquely about the strange turn in recent events. Especially with regards to Crystal returning from her vacation, then falling into a coma. It all happened so fast, that it still boggled him.

How had it ever come to this? One moment a man is celebrating the more cheerful aspects of his life, and the next instant, he is left to bemoan unthinkable grief and sorrow. He was a person that usually delighted in the simpler things, like spending time with the love of his life. Crystal really meant something to him, and added true value to his daily being- he had to have her!

Even a quiet sensation, like running his hands down the length of his lover's legs, would send thrills of pleasure throughout his body. Did women realize how much of a joy it was for a man to touch such silky, soft skin? Did they know just how therapeutic this was at the end of a long, hard day? Seeing Crystal's beautiful smile, then reaching over to caress her smooth shoulders, lifted his spirits and made his soul come alive. She was absolutely the centerpiece of his life.

Holding her in a tender embrace, planting seductive kisses on her neck, then listening to her coo to the warmth of his touch; these were the experiences that he secretly exalted. He'd already been employed more than 35 years in his lifetime, mostly with some of the seediest characters and toughest criminals in modern society. He had even been invited to some of the fanciest fêtes, thrown at many a prestigious estate. A big house is not a home, when it's filled with bitterness and hate. Crystal filled their home with joy and mirth.

In the past, Dellevega did treat himself to a few expensive toys over the years, like the BMW 750*i*. Those big-ticket rewards served as a constant reminder of how diligently he had worked and saved his money. Yet, at the end of the day, the brilliant shine of Crystal's beaming face, the bronzed glow of her supple skin, and the syrupy sweet tone with which she spoke to him lit his entire world on *FIRE!* He'd never known happiness before he had the grace to meet this angel.

Nothing in his existence would amount to a thing right now, if he didn't have her as an integral part of his universe. He didn't know what he had done to get so lucky in the lottery of life. He didn't know what he had done to earn her love. All he knew was that his time on this earth would be absolutely meaningless without her right there by his side each day. With Crystal, he'd finally discovered the definition of peace. His heart was filled with gladness that she'd chosen to align her destiny with his…

However fleeting.

For nothing lasts forever! Nothing in this life is a guarantee, except unto death. Now here Crystal laid, in a deep sleep of sorts. Unresponsive. Although there were some stirrings lately, no one knew when she would officially wake up and arise to assume the status of her original glory. Oh sure, he was told that she could end up becoming a vegetable, a mere shadow of her former self. He wasn't sure if he could handle that- if it did indeed happen that way. He made a commitment to take care of her until the bitter end. Sadly, hadn't he been down this road before? The emotionally draining journey of watching his first wife waste away from cancer a few years ago, nearly did his spirit in. This threatened to rob him of his zest for life.

It took a long time for Dellevega to fully recover. Now he was actually going through his days with a sense of awe and conscious awareness again. Before that, he was just walking around like an empty shell. A soul-less zombie with no feelings or emotions. *Then along came Crystal.* Dr. Crystal Knight-Davenport was how she had first introduced herself to him on that fateful day at the beach in his native land of Puerto Rico. As he shook her hand cordially, he remembered hearing her speak her name, but nothing more after that. He found himself in a daze while viewing this mesmerizing beauty, and longed to get to know her.

Oh, how he craved to hear her voice once more. His body ached for her stimulating hot oil massages, inspiring conversations, and the very essence of her being. Was it selfish of him to desperately want the object of his affections to re-animate and come back to life? Was it wrong of him to demand that she be able to continue feeding his carnal desires and meet his needs? Was it foolish to expect things to return back to normal again, or was he still entitled to his feelings?

At the moment, Detective Don Dellevega didn't care about 'right versus wrong.' He hadn't asked for much during his five-plus decades of time on this earth, but he was indeed asking for *this*. On a daily (sometimes hourly) basis he would get down on both his knees and pray for the safe return of his beloved. He prayed that Crystal would not go gently into that ol' good night. He just wasn't ready to let go of her yet. He couldn't take it if she made the transition during his absence, so he kept a constant vigil by her side. He continued to say his *novenas*, asking God to show a sign that his muse would come back to him somehow. He kept hope alive, if only to make it woefully through another day. He tried even harder to keep his wits about him.

Nothing else mattered right now. He hired a private nurse and had taken an extended leave of absence from his investigations job to care for Crystal in their home. His colleagues on the *Anti-Human Trafficking Task Force* were curious at first. What could be such an urgent family emergency during one of their most critical sting operations? However, once they found out that his mate had tried to singlehandedly take down the very same villain that they had spent years chasing all over the globe, they couldn't fill out the paperwork fast enough. Everyone was sending him their verbal support and condolences, but it was a little too premature for that. Because hey, this girl was a fighter!

Sure others in similar situations succumbed to their injuries and never made it back this way again. But not his girl. No, she was a warrior if ever there lived one. She had the strength of a samurai, the know-how of a ninja, and the mighty courage of a Serengeti lioness protecting her cubs. That child-murdering coward, Mr. Juan Rosario Ortega, had better run to the farthest corners of the earth. For now he had another sworn enemy with a serious pledge to terminate him.

Detective Don Dellevega had officially joined Crystal in her campaign to bring this reign of tyranny and terror to a swift end. He didn't care about his career these days, and had no fear for his own life. He knew that Ortega and his goons could have him marked for death, but that would not stop his pursuit of justice.

Before he was an officer of the law, he was trained as a soldier in the U.S. Army. Now here he was, declaring war on these infidels. If it was the last thing he would do, he'd get bloody revenge for his beloved Crystal.

Sangre por Sangre. Sangre por Sangre!

Blood for blood. Blood for blood!

PART TWO

"Not every storm in life is listed in the forecast."

Anonymous

CHAPTER 3

"I'm walking in the beauty of all that I am,
and all that I was born to be.
A shining example of God's grace and sheer majesty.
Through rainbows and butterflies,
Life's wicked lows and blissful highs...
Still cannot undo the sacredness of ME!"

What she really needed to do right now was learn to love herself. She felt her life spinning out of control and desperately wanted to anchor onto something solid, stable, and steady. Crystal needed some support.

The date was December 12, 1989 and Ms. Crystal Knight had an epiphany about her young existence. As the fifteen-year-old girl sat scribbling frantically in her journal, it occurred to her that only *she* had the power to control what happened to her from now on. Although she was currently a ward of the State of New York, residing for the next four months in a facility for juvenile delinquents, she was still a vulnerable human being with various thoughts, feelings, and emotions.

The problem was this: those same thoughts, feelings, and emotions were causing her to spiral down into a world of chaos and confusion. Thankfully, she was never one to experiment with mind-altering drugs. Yet this dubious streak of teen angst and rebellion was going to get her into a whole heap of trouble someday!

Succumbing to negative peer pressure, and pulling capricious pranks with her friends was starting to bring out the bad side of her. It even began to impact her performance in school. Her academic grades had always been counted on to be outstanding-now she was starting to slip in key subject areas. Her teachers expressed disappointment, but no one could seem to reach her. Emotionally, she was a firestorm of feelings. Mentally, she was in urgent need of some serious help.

And now it had come to this: juvenile delinquency.

But how exactly did she end up here, in this hell-hole? How did she land herself in such dire circumstances? The last thing she could actually remember before getting arrested was pushing through the wooden turnstiles at the Harlem 145th Street subway station with her best friend, Anne-Marie. It was such a stupid thing to do because she actually had the train fare (a 90 cent token) held tightly in the palm of her hand. All of a sudden, a burly transit cop appeared out of thin air.

Crystal turned around to look for her bossy little friend, but Anne-Marie was nowhere to be seen, having taken off running in the opposite direction. This left Crystal to fend for herself against the charges of fare evasion. When the police officer pulled out a pair of handcuffs, ostensibly to march her into the holding pen in a hidden back room, the situation escalated into a violent shoving match. After calling for back-up, Crystal was quickly subdued and hauled off to the nearest courtroom. Now she found herself fighting for freedom, all while striving to stay alive.

Of course, it didn't have to be this way. Earlier that year, she had watched the most amazing movie: *Dead Poets Society*, with acclaimed actor Robin Williams. It inspired her to 'carpe diem,' or seize the day to make something useful out of her time on this earth. Crystal knew that she had a very special gift, and truly wanted to leave her mark on society; but for whatever reason, she was acting out in malevolent defiance. Her worst personality traits were beginning to surface, charting a path to mayhem and destructive malice.

Everyone goes through a season of change and growth throughout the adolescent years, but this series of unfortunate events could possibly stain the remainder of her young life. She had the potential to do something remarkable with her time, yet here she sat locked up in a dark cold grey cement cell, allowing others in authority to determine her every second of the day. Her family seemed to be many miles away.

And so was her sanity, her precious peace of mind. That's because she didn't belong here. No, she really didn't fit in, because *she wasn't one of them*. Why, she could hear them even now. Right through the very door. Heathens and hooligans howling loudly off in the distance. Demonic souls running through the hallways, hell bent on trouble-making and spreading pandemonium. Delirious young girls screaming like banshees in the cafeteria and common areas. These were the same demented hoodlums that jumped Crystal on her first day here. They stole her gold jewelry and robbed her of some fancy designer shoes.

Although she had a burgeoning interest in martial arts, (taking karate classes since the age of ten), it was still hard to fight them all off at the same time. And the way they duped her was such a set-up! Pretending to invite her to join them in a round of playing *double-dutch*, four of the biggest girls abruptly dropped the heavy ropes, then came rushing at her simultaneously.

After delivering a scathing round of kicks, blows, bites and scratches, Crystal barely escaped with her life. She knew better than to trust anyone after that initiation, and was actually glad to be sequestered in her cell. Since that incident, she remained isolated away from the general population; moping around her unit in a sullen, morose, and decidedly self-reflective mood.

Although she wanted to cry at the thought of someone else wearing her expensive Italian suede moccasins, Crystal was willing to let those trinkets go in return for a little safety and security. Oddly enough, *she* was the one who ended up in trouble for the rowdy noonday scuffle. Despite the four bullies clearly attacking her in front of the pre-occupied facility staff, Crystal was put into solitary confinement for two weeks. Well, at first she loved it- less tension and friction to endure!

Deep down she knew how beneficial this time alone would be for her. She somehow felt like her life was already in the process of changing for the better. As she entered her cell for an extended period, she was undoubtedly entering into a chrysalis of sorts. In her private little cocoon, she began the process of a giant transformation. She had no choice but to confront her inner demons and battle those unhealthy impulses and urges that had ruled her young life up until that point. She knew that the danger lied in being out of control, and desperately wanted to reverse the process. Crystal earnestly wished to make wiser choices; so she started by trying to envision a brighter future for herself- one with successful achievement and positive opportunity.

What doesn't kill you, makes you stronger! Indeed, she had already become something of an introverted loner, especially after the brutal killing of her revered older sister, Kim. So she was accustomed to enjoying a few pensive moments of deep thinking and quiet contemplation. She routinely talked to herself, and wasn't too shy to be caught visibly muttering various thoughts and revelations as she slinked down the hallway towards evening mealtime or morning showers. Nowadays, Crystal didn't care who was watching her, or spreading rumors that she was crazy.

This facet of her developing character eventually served to strengthen her resolve, and she became a more effective fighter. Crystal gained a reputation for being a ruthless warrior, a true force to be reckoned with. To defend herself, she would grab and use any object laying around nearby: steel chairs, table lamps, heavy textbooks, stiff hairbrushes. The other girls took notice, and grew tired of the painful bruises that a rousing encounter with Crystal would surely bring.

The other inmates of the facility were all like 'crabs in a barrel,' with a ghetto mentality to match. Their deplorable behavior made it hard to concentrate on academic studies. Even though the guards mostly ignored the young misfits, the teachers continued to struggle with maintaining order and discipline in their classrooms. All, that is, except one.

Like a gift from the instructional gods, one pedagogue reigned supreme in Crystal's social consciousness, as this incredible saint helped to transform her into the refined young lady that she was yet to become.

CHAPTER 4

At the end of the week, Crystal woke up with a smile on her face, because today was Freaky Friday. That meant that everyone got to watch the most popular television shows in the shared common area: *Baywatch*, *90210*, *Saved By the Bell*, *A Different World*, *Family Matters*, *Seinfeld*, *American Gladiators*, and re-runs of her own personal favorite, *Fame*. This also meant, unfortunately, that there would be a lot of fighting for who could control changing the channels.

As her fellow inmates argued loudly over who last had the pliers to turn the missing knob, while fiddling with the aluminum foil-wrapped-hanger-replaced-antenna to get better reception, Crystal sat quietly staring at the TV with a blank expression. She was daydreaming about the bucolic scenes that she routinely saw flashing across the screen during the daytime shows.

In vivid colors of kelly green and azure blue, she gazed upon the pristine beaches of Santa Monica. With not one visible cloud in the sky, it seemed to never rain in Southern California. Or at least, not in lovely Los Angeles County. It occurred to Crystal that she had become obsessed with a beautiful place that she'd never been to, but would be delighted to visit someday.

How wonderful it would be to take a nice, long drive up into the mountains along the Pacific Coast Highway. She wished she could be on one of those pristine white beaches, watching in awe as the gnarly surfer dudes hang ten on a rockin' monster wave. *Kowabunga!*

Thinking about the chilly winter drafts that invaded her tiny cell in upstate New York, it seemed to Crystal that the good life was so very, very far away. She secretly wanted to be Malibu Barbie, lounging around luxuriously with Ken in a convertible- with nothing but sunshine and chandeliers for the rest of her days.

Except she wasn't some plastic Malibu Barbie doll, and no Ken was coming to the rescue to bail her out of this shady circumstance. To prove this fact, a random spitball flying upside her head interrupted her reverie. It served as a reminder that she was still locked up in a girl's penitentiary slash mental institution. As the guilty party snickered suspiciously, Crystal sighed and slowly began to plot her escape. She knew that if she was going to stay sane, she had to get out of this place!

Sometimes she wished she could just turn invisible and disappear from sight- that way people would have to leave her alone. Not only would she be able to walk through walls; if they couldn't see her, then maybe they wouldn't pick on her so much. She knew she was different from the others, but didn't quite realize what it was that made her so special. Why did her presence require so much extra attention from the other girls if she was deliberately remaining quiet all the time? She knew better than to run around instigating drama, so choosing to play deaf and mute seemed like a strategy.

Remembering the lyrics to Michael Jackson's smash hit *"Beat It"* Crystal wanted to stand her ground, but grew tired of having to fight off these demons every single day. Occasionally, she caught herself drifting off into a fantasy world where she mysteriously woke up with mutant superhero powers. She even likened herself to one of the courageous *X-Men* she always read about in the comic books. As a lone crusader, she would rally against the forces of evil and bring about a sense of justice, fairness, and balance to this world.

Although she had made some mistakes in her life, she would make sure that her stay in this facility would not become permanent. Crystal Knight didn't know much yet in her young life, but she knew one thing for sure- she had to BREAK OUT! Day by day, this became her own secret *Mission Impossible*. To fill the hours, she spent her time plotting and planning on how she would make her great escape. This scheming usually alternated with her other favorite pastime: longing to live in a nicer place with a warm year-round climate.

In her dreams, Crystal convinced herself that she could live the rich life of the famous celebrities that she saw happily prancing around on the television screen. As she lay on her cot, she imagined those cool Santa Ana winds blowing in over the coastal expanse of the Pacific Ocean. At night, gently caressing breezes would softly wash over her as she laid flat on her back and stared idly up at the constellations in a starry sky.

Wiggling her toes in the powdery beach sand, she'd leisurely listen to the soothing lullaby of lazily lapping waves crashing against the shore. Picking up loose seashells and rummaging for metamorphic rocks would become her new hobby. In addition, all year round she'd delight in eating yummy caramel ice cream cones and salt water taffy on the lively Santa Monica Pier. Then during the mystical full moon, her ears would prick up to detect the distant howl of hungry wolves, mountain lions, raccoons, and wild coyotes in Topanga State Park. That would be so cool!

Instead, here she was locked up in a penitentiary enduring frigid Siberian temps with these deranged, drama-driven, power-hungry foxes. Each one more territorial than the next. Tops on their agenda, was roaming the vast grounds of the female correctional facility, looking for every opportunity to instigate a fight. They were like a coven of witches: a demented breed that actually thrived on promoting violent confrontations. Mercilessly stalking their prey and casting a wide net to ensnare all unwilling participants.

No matter how much Crystal and the adult staff members tried to ignore this evil gang, they would try their utmost best to brew up some negative conflict.

Energy vampires. Drama queens. Attention whores.

Not a single one of them could go a full hour in solitary confinement without threatening to destroy the premises or cursing the staff with turmoil and chaos. Whenever a 'tough one' was restrained, there was much wailing and gnashing of teeth heard on the ward.

However there was strength in numbers, and this legion of hellions was beginning to grow by the day. Their trickery and tomfoolery tested the patience of the cafeteria staff; constantly befuddling the on-site nurse, state psychologist, and the youth development aides.

There simply was nowhere to run, *nowhere to hide*. The building itself was full of long, narrow hallways that ended in small, cramped spaces. The real trouble-makers knew every last nook and cranny of the facility, so there wasn't even a quantum of solace to be had for concentrating on clearing one's head. Although male juvenile delinquents were successfully ushered through their common areas, silently marching lockstep in single file, the female facility was a completely different scenario: there was no discipline.

It was nearly impossible to enforce the Auburn system of conformity with these out-of-control young ladies. Whether it was due to mental illness, emotional instability, hormonal imbalances, or just a plain lack of good home training- the girls seemed to be running the place instead of the staff. All that was, except for The Warden. He had his cruel, under-handed, cold-hearted ways of punishing all young offenders who refused to follow the penal code of the juvenile justice system.

On the bus ride coming in, young Crystal had spied the endless thicket of dense forestry that seamlessly surrounded the property on all sides. Escaping seemed like such a daunting task, but she could care less. She wasn't concerned about getting caught, or the threat of failing to survive in the freezing winter cold and miles of widespread wilderness. All she knew was that she didn't belong here, and she had to break out!

Somehow...

CHAPTER 5

Coming towards the end of her solitary confinement, Crystal was slowly starting to lose her mind. As much as she thought of herself as a loner on these premises, she discovered that she did indeed need somebody to talk to! Much to her chagrin, she longed for the days when she was laughing uncontrollably with her little buddy, Ariel Basquez. Whether they were discussing the latest teen TV shows, or trading beauty secrets, Ariel was the bubbly bit of sunshine that lit up Crystal's day. She was just a cool person to hang with.

Now that Ariel was gone, there was really no one else to converse with or gravitate towards. Nobody else held that fascination for Crystal; no one at the facility was quite as talkative, lively, or entertaining as Ariel. She had a friendly smile, goofy personality, and a warm spirit that just made you want to spend time with her. When Ariel was around, the hours just seemed to fly by effortlessly. Soon it would be time to go to bed.

By contrast, doing jail time without a good friend around to provide support, was proving to be harder than putting contact lenses on a fidgety-azz cat: one moment Crystal thought she had a solid grasp on her sanity and the next minute she was climbing the walls!

inside she was confused and nonplussed. *How many more of these venomous attacks would she have to fend off during her short stay here?* And why was it that as the victim of continued injustices, she always seemed to be the one getting into trouble? She couldn't understand this.

Nurse Brown busily scrubbed down the main counter with ammonia, then began to tidy up the various accoutrements tucked away in the cabinets. As an obsessive-compulsive neat freak, her environment was never deemed sterile enough. The noxious fumes from the disinfectant often made even the hypochondriacs sicker than when they first came in. *Everything must be clean, clean, clean, clean, clean!* This was her mantra, and was loudly repeated to anyone who visited the tiny clinic (which prompted most people to scram).

Ms. Ligurio stood guard by the front door, lips pursed and arms crossed, looking like she was about to deliver the speech of a lifetime. Crystal already knew that her mentor expected much better from her, and felt ashamed of her heated over-reaction and bold rage. But before Ms. Ligurio could begin to express disappointment over Crystal's lack of self-control, two more people entered into the diminutive waiting room.

Crystal looked up from her downtrodden state of mind. The state psychologist, Ms. Kristen Thompkins, had decided to join in on their conversation. She was accompanied by a very tall, big-boned female that Crystal had never set eyes on before. Larger than life, she was an amazon of a creature, a visitor who seemed to take up whatever space that remained in the room.

Dr. Thompkins cleared her throat, then signaled that she fully intended to interrupt the rousing discussion:

"Nurse Brown, this is the one. This is the new girl I was telling you about. The patient's name is Scheherazade Taylor, also known as Sherry T. I need you to tend to her first."

"Oh, I'm so sorry that you had to experience that, my dear. Honestly, my heart goes out to you. I sincerely sympathize with all you've had to go through since then, and I wish I could've been there to protect you."

Ms. Ligurio glanced nervously over at Dr. Thompkins, feeling like she was treading on thin ice and venturing into unchartered territory. Realizing that talk therapy didn't always lead to emotional clarity, she paused to gather her thoughts before finding just the right words.

Proceeding in a softer, lower tone of voice, Ms. Ligurio continued with her lecture: "Listen Crystal, I want to tell you that you are a giraffe, not an anteater."

Curious as where this discourse was leading to, Dr. Thompkins shifted silently in her chair. Psychological counseling was supposed to be her domain of expertise, but Ms. Ligurio had a healing persona that appeared to help many of the young ladies in recovery.

"Always remember this, Crystal. You were born to be very different from these other girls. You are a star! You are bright, intelligent, well-spoken, possess good hygiene habits, and you're a talented dancer, as well."

Crystal began to perk up and pay closer attention to what Ms. Ligurio was saying. No one had ever heaped so many accolades upon her all at once. Sure, a few boys had told her that she was cute, but she never had such a lifting boost to her confidence and self-esteem.

Ms. Ligurio proceeded with her analogy: "You know that a giraffe eats exclusively from the treetops, being entitled to the choicest of leaves and foliage; whereas an anteater roots around on the ground, digging up dirt and shoving its nose everywhere looking for its food."

"That's right, but it's not really an issue of one animal being better the other, just different. They both have their needs met, but in different ways." Ms. Ligurio shot Dr. Thompkins a sideways glare for interrupting, then resumed so Crystal could get the idea of the story:

"Giraffes are definitely seen as more graceful, and are biologically designed with long necks to reach the very tippy tippy tops of the trees around them. Now they really can't buck evolution, and one day decide that they want to go against function, and scavenge around on the ground near the roots instead. First of all, they wouldn't fit in with the rest of the crowd doing that.

Second, they could end up choking themselves to death trying to swallow their food in that awkward position, just for adopting someone else's style. If you know that you were born to be a giraffe, carry yourself accordingly. Hold your neck up high, and let your graceful carriage speak for itself. Don't bother to belittle yourself, trying to scrounge around on the dirty ground. Let these other girls be anteaters, while you rise above the fray, plucking the juiciest leaves from the tops of trees. Get the gist of what I'm saying?" Ms. Ligurio sat back, giving her words time to sink in.

As her eyes lit up with revelation, young Crystal slowly nodded her head in agreement. She had just had an epiphany about who she was truly meant to be.

Why was she letting these satanic demons drain her energy today, when she had a big performance tomorrow? This was her spotlight. This was her time to shine! When Nurse Brown and Sherry T. finally emerged from the examination room, Crystal was looking up and beaming proudly. When asked why she was so happy all of a sudden, she simply replied:

"I just found out that I'm a giraffe, not an anteater!"

Everyone in the room erupted into laughter, except the new girl, who had yet to hear the good news about being "different" and socially unique. Crystal kindly offered to enlighten her on the way back to their cells.

As they walked down the long hallway together, totally engrossed in conversation, they suddenly heard a loud BOOM! Feeling the after-effects of a mini bomb blast ricochet through the building, the girls instantly became shaken and startled. With piercing fire alarms blaring, they followed the rehearsed drills and quickly lined up to exit at the front of the facility.

Although most of the girls were only wearing sweatshirts and shorts, everyone was pushed to the outer perimeter of the compound, while waiting for the fire trucks to arrive. A fresh new pack of snow had fallen recently, but the young inmates were still forced to stand around in their sneakers and flip-flop slippers.

While standing around in the freezing temps of the wintery Siberian Express, a shivering Crystal resisted the temptation to vapidly indulge in loud complaining. Instead, she looked around carefully, surveying her Upstate New York surroundings and devising a plan.

Crystal didn't know whether she was born to be a giraffe or not; but there was one thing she did know: that she would be busting out of this place soon. And perhaps she just met the one person who could help make it all happen!

CHAPTER 8

It was Christmas Eve, but instead of opening up gifts underneath a huge bedazzled tree in the warmth of her family's home, Crystal was running laps around the border of the facility grounds. As she kept pace ahead of the other girls, crunching ice pellets with Adidas tennis shoes, she could feel her outer extremities begin to numb with frostbite. At least she was lucky enough to have had on her usual pink woolly fingerless gloves.

True, she had her Sony Walkman headphones to give her running some rhythm. However, it was abundantly clear that all of the young inmates were woefully under-dressed to still be outside in a sub-zero climate.

A million silly thoughts shot through Crystal's mind:

-How did Fatima get a blanket to avoid hypothermia?

-Why is it that the staff members were conversing and smoking cigarettes while the girls were catching cold?

-If the fire had already been put out twenty minutes ago, what were they doing running laps like maniacs?

-With all of the busy traffic coming down the hill, why was The Warden standing so close to that highway?

Crystal kept up her stride, while also keeping up her surveillance of the security measures at the front gate.

Located a few miles from the nearest residential town, and nestled amongst secluded mountainous peaks, the sprawling grounds of the juvenile facility sat at the base of a steep hill. The road just outside the steel gates was actually a thruway which was popular with long-distance truck drivers, and speeding motorists taking a short-cut route through the expansive valley.

In fact, rumor had it that the YDAs were so lax about escapees because if the timber wolves didn't kill you, then trying to cross the street surely would. The steady stream of cars zooming by was nonstop, day and night. Still, a few young females had tried, but to no avail. The terrifying terrain usually made them come back in.

Once Crystal and the other girls were hustled back into the building, there was another rude awakening: no hot tea was available, only cold dry cereal for dinner. The showers only had cold water, the hot water had been shut off. Lastly, the highly anticipated Christmas party was canceled. Reportedly, a certain someone started a grease fire in the kitchen just because the facility ran out of her favorite afternoon snack. That was the problem with selfish people who lacked self-control, they didn't think about the consequences of their actions and always messed things up for everyone else.

Crystal dove under the thin covers on her cot, trying not to catch pneumonia, but still had trouble falling asleep. The facility went into full lock-down mode for the second time in two weeks, so there was no movement allowed in the hallways. Also, none of the girls could sneak over into another inmate's cell, as friends were accustomed to doing during the evening hours. It was too early to call 'lights out,' so Crystal decided to fetch Ariel's diary and read a bit; since that would be better than being alone and bored to death.

Flipping through the pages, it was clear that her bestie was at a point in her life where she was having a lot of problems at home. Poor Ariel was unhappy about her relationship with her mother, a single-parent who was trying to raise her with a strict hand of discipline and tough love. They were having a lot of arguments concerning what time she should come home from school to study and complete her homework. Add to that the fact that she was spending a lot of nights out at her boyfriend's house; the two teens were high school sweethearts but her Mom didn't really approve of him.

After browsing through a couple of scribbled pages that mostly featured complaints about the harshness of her mother, there was one particular journal entry that immediately caught Crystal's eye:

Now what am I gonna do?

I met this pretty girl, named Jezebel, that I thought was in high school just like me. She came up to me at the mall, and asked my opinion about this dress she was trying on. It looked a little skanky to me, but I said it was sexy and we started to talk. She seemed kinda cool, so when she insisted that we go for hot chocolate afterwards, I didn't think nothing of it. Later on that week, she started calling my cell phone and blowing me up on Facebook like crazy. I didn't mind cuz I kinda liked all the extra attention I was gettin'.

Then she invited me to a party at her older friend's house. I thought about it, cuz it was on a school nite, but my mom's been getting on my last nerve lately. Even though she told me not to go, I still wanted to have some fun. That day, I took a change of clothes to school, then went to the address that the girl gave me. I knew deep down inside that it was wrong to disobey my mother like that, but the chick said that everyone would be there. My boyfriend has been very buzy doing something else these days, so he ain't around too much to hang with me like before. I guess I was just feeling kinda lonely and rejected when she came along...

At that point, the YDAs came around to enforce the curfew, so Crystal tucked the diary underneath her pillow, with a solid resolve to finish some more of it the next day. When she awoke in the morning, she took yet another artic shower, ate some Cookie Crisp cereal, then scurried back to her unit. Scheherazade stopped by to say 'Merry Christmas' and to ask her to hang out in the main lounge area, but Crystal declined-recounting the events of the previous day. She just wanted to be left alone so she could read more about Ariel's thoughts during the last days of her short life.

But why did this have to happen to me? Why?

When I got to the place where the party was being held, it looked run-down and shabby. Something told me at the last minute not to go inside, but I didn't listen to my gut instinct. I was about to turn around and walk away, but Jezebel came out and convinced me to come inside. She placed an open beer bottle in my hand and said they were expecting a lot of cute guys to show up. I mostly just saw creepy older men there. When I drank the beer, I started to feel kinda woozy, then I blacked out.

Later on, I woke up in the basement of the house handcuffed to a filthy bed. Jezebel told me that this was my new home and that I shouldn't try to escape, or else they would just find me and kill my whole family. She told me that I would be a sex slave from now on, but not to worry because I would learn to like it. After a while, a man came in the room and made me call him "Daddy." He said that I was his special little doll, and they gave me a Barbie tattoo across my belly button. He said this was to brand me with a label showing that I belonged to him.

Shocked by what she was reading, Crystal endeavored to finish the whole journal in one sitting; but she paused when she heard a stern knock on the metal door. At first she tried to ignore it, but then she heard the clang of a thousand keys jangling. Immediately she jumped up and rushed to put Ariel's diary away, fearing that the YDAs would confiscate it as illegal contraband, if they ever found it in her possession...

CHAPTER 9

In her haste to scramble over to the door, Crystal forgot that she was only wearing a little cotton bra top and skimpy pink panties while in bed. When she flung open the door, she was surprised to see who was standing there- surprised, but really not pleased. The Warden was alone and stood stock still, eyes drinking in the virginal freshness of her nubile body and supple skin. Instantly embarrassed, Crystal tried to slam the door shut, but he quickly jammed his left foot in it.

With an evil grin, he leered at her squirming in shame and discomfort: "Young lady, come with me. I believe we have some unfinished business to be settled today."

Crystal felt herself about to burst into tears. She already heard rumors about certain girls, who once selected, randomly disappeared for hours then received special privileges from him afterwards. She didn't know why he was so intent on doing her harm, and tried to figure out whether she should yell for help, or stomp on his foot, then wedge herself against the door.

Looking around to see if one of her guardian angels would come to her rescue, she remembered that it was time for a scheduled change of shift on a Saturday afternoon: a key period when there were no facility staff members hanging around to check up on the girls.

The Warden continued to smile smugly, knowing that Crystal couldn't get away. On a holiday such as this, it's a wonder that anyone made it in to work. Most had called out sick, leaving the facility short-staffed.

All wanted to have their holiday at home, except one:

"*Je-sus, take the wheel!* Lord, it's a mess out there in that blizzard; I'm lucky I even made it through the snow. So now, which lucky volunteer would like to help me with housekeeping duties?" Nurse Brown's boisterous voice could be heard all down the corridor.

Seizing the opportunity, Crystal screamed out: "*I do!*"

Nurse Brown's corpulent form came careening around the corner, Electrolux in hand. The Warden, sensing a checkmate, quipped "Cynthia, I thought you called out today. What are you doing here on a quiet Christmas?"

"Child, the work ever needs to get done. I couldn't have my little pickneys running around with the flu. I brought in some extra cough medicine, just in case."

Crystal took advantage of the distraction to softly close the door, while still shouting that she wanted to vacuum the facility with Nurse Brown. When she finally emerged fully dressed in regulation uniform, she was relieved to see that The Warden had disappeared. Happily humming while performing her cleaning chores, she thanked her lucky stars for grace.

Having completed her vacuuming and mopping chores to Nurse Brown's satisfaction, it was now time for Crystal's little treat.

One of the private luxuries that the nurse bestowed upon her favorites was a smoothie blended with fresh strawberries, ripe bananas, yogurt, and a drizzle of sweet honey on top. Pure indulgence.

It seemed like no one else would be coming into the clinic for a while, so Crystal took advantage of the lull.

"Nurse Brown, can I please talk to you a minute about something serious that's been on my mind alot lately?"

"Sure child, sit down and take a load off, you deserve it; I've been meaning to have a chat with you anyway."

"Really, and what did I do now?" Crystal didn't comprehend why these older folks were so keen to keep on preaching to her about high moral standards.

"Don't go getting all defensive on me, child. I just wanted to say a few words about your growing reputation for being a fighter and a little trouble-maker around here. But, I suspect that this isn't the real you."

"Well, I don't care what people say about me. The truth is, I'm innocent. The actual trouble-makers are the other girls who're always starting crap with me."

"Yeah that may be so, but don't let other people change you on the cellular level. Don't let their evil DNA invade your genetics and turn you into a vampire just like them. I've observed that you are an intelligent young lady and you hail from superior stock, so start acting like it." Nurse Brown asserted in a serious tone.

"Now how am I supposed to carry myself like a lady in a place full of deranged hooligans? I was brought here on a fare-evasion charge and I find myself locked up with teenagers who are already hardened criminals!"

"Hey that's no excuse. Look at me; I've been working here for nearly thirty-eight years, and I haven't let this madness change my personality one bit. Not one bit!"

"Wow, thirty-eight years. That's like a life sentence!"

"Yep, and I'll tell you how I did it. I always remember what my parents taught me about preserving a good character. Character is your usual manner of behavior. It's who you truly are, on the inside. Therefore, it's not about what other people think of you, it's how you actually view yourself. When you don't view yourself as a wild animal, you refuse to act like one in public."

"Okay, so I hear what you're saying, and to a certain degree, understand that it's my responsibility to control my own behavior at all times. However, if I wasn't taught all this by my parents, then how do I decide a course of action to take in a given scenario?"

"This goes back to your inherent moral standards and virtues. It relies on the innate ability of every human being to know right from wrong. Virtue is a humble, yet voluntary, obedience to live according to the word of God, and to always do the right thing in any kind of tricky situation." Nurse Brown smiled benevolently.

"So if the other girls here can choose to do good, over constantly being evil, then why don't they?" Crystal was confused as to what made her so special and rare.

"Some of these girls have only been exposed to abuse, poverty, and ignorance their whole lives. However, I read your profile and you come from a totally different background. You have suffered childhood trauma, but that doesn't make you a violent person by default."

"And what about Ariel Basquez? There doesn't seem to be any investigation going on to solve her untimely death. She wasn't a violent type of person either."

"True, but she made some unfortunate decisions that just snowballed into one huge tragedy after another. She didn't weigh the consequences of her choices, and eventually they all caught up with her in a bad way."

"And it doesn't help that some adults took advantage of her, using her innocence and defiance to trick her with misinformation, based upon wicked intentions!"

"Yes ma'am. Including one or two predatory adults located right here on these very premises. I can't give you any further details or answers, but I can offer you some lollipops in return for helping me clean up here."

Crystal thanked Nurse Brown for the additional sweets, then slowly made her way back to her cell, unescorted by any YDAs. Her brain was buzzing with this latest conversation, as she relished the fact that there were still people who cared enough about her safety, to want to see her successful and doing well.

Perhaps it had turned out to be a Merry Christmas, after all…

CHAPTER 10

Will I ever get out of this gang life, will I ever escape?
Or was I born to be forced into prostitution and rape...

Crystal could not stop reading the compelling diary of her friend, the late Ariel Basquez. Each entry turned out to be more jaw-dropping than the last. She found herself gripped in the throes of curiosity, unable to put the book down. Determined to get to the bottom of the mystery surrounding her buddy's death, Crystal scanned the pages for clues about her whereabouts in the final few hours before she was discovered hanging.

Normally, young Crystal would be claustrophobic being confined to such a small space over any length of time. While she was appreciative of the fact that each female inmate had her own room, and a metal door to lock behind them to stave off unwanted vices like petty theft, she still felt the walls closing in on her.

She was usually the avid daydreamer, sitting by the windows in class, looking for sunshine and trying to gauge how the weather was at that particular moment.

Yet here she was in her windowless cell, hunkered down and totally engrossed in someone else's troubles; reading the salacious detail of where it all went wrong.

Apparently, Ariel was moved from the basement of the first house, to a motel where she was part of a stable of other kidnapped teenage girls. Most of the other victims were kept high on drugs like weed, cocaine and heroin- each one taking turns to satisfy the pimp daddy, in addition to a nonstop flow of male clients.

According to the journal, Ariel was sequestered in a private, secluded upstate New York location, and forced to service upwards of twenty men a day. She, along with four other unlucky ladies, brought in approximately $800 daily. Their handler (known as 'the manager') paid for their food, tampons, upkeep, condoms and lodging. Occasionally he took them all shopping for new clothes at the local mall. On these rare outings, they would be given about $100 each. While this was framed as an earned reward, it still seemed like a paltry sum for all of the work required.

Crystal paused her reading, and quickly did the mental math: ($800 x 5 girls x 300 days) and came up with a whopping total of $1.2 million dollars a year in tax-free income! Whoa! And they say *crime doesn't pay*.

Ariel fell in love with her pimp because she never had a father figure around when she was growing up. Also, he was from the same Latino background as her, so she felt they had their shared language in common.

However, even with the strict control with which he ruled over her, and the subsequent camaraderie that she enjoyed with the girls, Ariel still devised a plan to escape the situation she precariously found herself in. She slit a small hole in the lining of her bra, and started putting tips from her gentlemen callers away in the push-up padding. For safe keeping. For a rainy day. That way, when she was ordered to strip down and hand over her earnings, it would not be detected.

Eventually, she was able to run away and hitch a ride to the nearest bus depot. Unfortunately, upon reaching Port Authority in New York City in the middle of the day, she was picked up by police for traveling without identification. Since she was under-aged and gave them a phony name, they sent her to juvenile court. Although her advocate explained to the judge about the dire circumstances surrounding her recent activity, she was speedily convicted and sentenced to nine months at this upstate residential facility. Poor Ariel!

But the biggest surprise had yet to be revealed. For imagine how dumbfounded she was when upon arrival on her first day, she discovered that one of her regular customers was actually a prominent employee at the facility. They recognized each other instantly! He had a penchant for making her dress up in a cheerleader costume, and calling him 'Coach.' What a sick puppy.

Ariel vowed to keep his dirty little secret, in exchange for certain little treats and privileges, of course. However, his demands grew tiring, as he insisted on meeting her at all hours of the day and night, at the run-down tool shed out in the back yard. Where the gardening equipment was kept. There, she had to do his every bidding on a filthy mattress on the bare floor.

Lately, she was making up excuses for not meeting him there. In all actuality, she had caught the eye of one of the handsome YDAs that just joined the staff a few weeks prior. As the youngest person on payroll, he was paying her copious

CHAPTER 11

Later on that night, Crystal woke up in tears after suffering through yet another bad dream. This time it was a strange nightmare that begged to be deciphered, explained, and interpreted to her young mind. As startling as this scary episode was, she did not realize that it also had prophetic overtones. Although she was left dazed and confused, this dream was a prescient vision of what was actually still to come in her future:

Crystal was standing in her high school science laboratory admiring a baby squid that was being held in a large, clear open container fully on display. She heard one of the adult lab assistants enter the room, and turned to address him. There were no other students coming into the cavernous space, and all was strangely quiet. When she turned back around, it appeared that the cephalopod had metastasized into a giant octopus. She blinked her eyes in utter disbelief.

Surprised by the instant transformation, she warned the lab assistant to not go near the open container. He sarcastically smirked at her protests, and insisted that it was just her imagination. As he smugly approached the vessel to show her how harmless the beast was, a long sinewy tentacle began to unfurl and extend out.

Suddenly, the huge specimen turned into a growling monster and inched itself slowly up, towards the very top of the container. While the lab assistant stood facing her and jestering, the hungry beast grew exponentially. Lurching forward, it wrapped its multiple tentacles around the chest cavity of the young man and lifted him straight up into the air. As he fought and yelled vehemently to be released, the mammoth creature quickly stuffed his entire person into the waiting portal that was its vast mouth. Head, torso, and legs all disappeared into the gobbling hole.

Crystal shrieked hysterically and turned to run out of the room. Just then, she heard the science teacher walking along in the hallway. Crystal paused her exit momentarily to warn her not to enter into the classroom. As the teacher stood there bewildered, trying to figure out exactly what Crystal was ranting about, a giant tentacle came out and wrapped tightly around the woman's throat. As she tried to escape its deadly chokehold, it snatched her body jerkily back into the classroom. Now Crystal was determined to run out of the building to avoid being the next victim.

She hastily turned around, coming face to face with the massive, bulbous, slithering form of the greedily devouring leviathan. She tried to scream for help, but no words came to her mouth, so she stood transfixed...

Crystal woke up, like on many other occasions, in a heated sweat. She had also been screaming at the top of her lungs, unbeknownst to her. In fact, the overnight staff of YDAs was so accustomed to these midnight terrors that they impatiently banged on her cell door, reminding her that other people were actually trying to get some sleep. Unsympathetic to her servitude that was routinely imposed upon the inmates. *Didn't she already mop the floors?*

"Father, for many years I have been tortured by a hideous dream and tormented by an unnerving vision."

She briefly filled him in on the intimate details of the abduction of her sister, in the dark deserted woods at the tender age of eight years old. Fighting back the tears, she described the anguish of not being able to warn Kim, or protect her from impending harm. Although it happened late at night, on a camping trip during a family vacation, Crystal could still see the man who attacked her sister. He held a large object in his hand, then bashed Kim over the head until she fell.

Visibly moved to compassion when he heard about her plight, Father O'Riley sought to make sense of the whole sordid ordeal. However, Crystal cut straight to the point and demanded to know what God thought about her *insatiable need to exact revenge* on the man.

CHAPTER 12

Father O'Riley shifted uncomfortably in his chair as he stared momentarily out of the sole window in the bare room. Satisfied that he could amply provide Crystal with a solid answer, he retrieved an old King James bible and proceeded to rapidly turn the worn out pages.

"Well my little one, I will endeavor my best to assist you in this journey of truth. According to the tried and tested word of God, there is only one thing you can do- forgive! I know it will be a very hard thing at first..."

Crystal stared silently at the blushing priest, blinking slowly before she hesitantly spoke her true intentions:

"Father, let me confess. I keep having these bad thoughts that center around me hurting someone soon. I'm not only struggling with the urge to exact revenge against the man who kidnapped my sister ten years ago, I'm also dealing with this harrowing nightmare!"

"Oh dear! Oh my! Well, let's see. They didn't quite prepare me for this at the seminary school, but I do know three biblical verses about God's sense of divine justice. If you're interested, I could even write them down for you. It might prove helpful to remember later when you are fighting the temptation to do harm."

He pulled out a pad of paper and a Montblanc pen, then proceeded to busily scribble several appropriate lines from different chapters. Crystal stared aimlessly out the window, noting that once again The Warden was outside smoking cigarettes and socializing by the highway, instead of supervising the girls' activity. It didn't seem to matter however, because she soon heard them trudging back in from the yard like a herd of cattle. A staff member peeked into the room and told Crystal that her time was up and to go see The Warden.

Appearing to disobey a direct order, Crystal instead took the small sheet of paper from the priest and read quickly the assortment of biblical passages concerning the human quest for revenge. They also revealed God's sovereign power of righteousness and ultimate forgiveness of sin:

Deuteronomy 32:35

"To me belongeth vengeance, and recompence; their foot shall slide in due time; for the day of their calamity is at hand, and the things that shall come upon them make haste."

Proverbs 20:22

"Say not thou, I will recompense evil; but wait on the Lord, and he shall save thee."

Romans 12:19

"Dearly beloved, avenge not yourselves, but rather give place unto wrath: for it is written, Vengeance is mine; I will repay, saith the Lord."

<u>1 John 1:9</u>

"If we confess our sins, he is faithful and just to forgive us our sins, and to cleanse us from all unrighteousness."

<u>Ephesians 1:7</u>

"In whom we have redemption through his blood, the forgiveness of sins, according to the riches of his grace..."

<u>Isaiah 1:18</u>

"Come now, and let us reason together, saith the Lord: though your sins be as scarlet, they shall be as white as snow; though they be red like crimson, they shall be as wool."

***

Crystal hastily tucked the verses away in her bosom for safekeeping, knowing that the YDA was supposed to confiscate all notes being passed around. Before she left, the priest reminded her that God was able to "abundantly pardon a sinner and have compassion, as long as he or she was willing to forsake their previously wicked ways." Crystal thanked him for the sage advice, then prepared to be escorted by the YDA.

Back in the hallway, they were accompanied by the other missing truant, Ms. Sherry T. She appeared to be in an extremely agitated state, railing on and on about how much she hated this facility and wanting to leave.

Crystal listened quietly to her fellow inmate's griping, but internally, she was still digesting what the priest had said about the forgiveness of sin. It bothered her immensely to see people doing evil things to innocent children. She knew about the principle that *you reap what you sow.* She also knew that it was part of her devout Christian upbringing to "forgive others their trespasses," even as she asked God to forgive her own.

She was still wrestling with all of these divergent ideas when they went to see The Warden. Here was a man that Crystal had absolutely no regard or respect for whatsoever! Not an ounce. She despised everything about him already, however since reading Ariel's diary she had grown to detest him uncontrollably. He took one look at Scheherazade Taylor's pissed-off face, and directed the YDA to take her angry behind back inside.

This was despite Crystal's pleading objection…

Once they were alone, The Warden began winking at Crystal and bombarding her with lewd insinuations laced with blatantly sexual overtones. Crystal danced around, shivering and watching the early setting of the winter sun. As she blocked out his ongoing banter, she began to take stock of such a beautiful surrounding.

The urban landscape was completely covered in snow. Pristine crystals covered the entire terrain with a glistening white blanket that sparkled in the dusk light.

Far off in the horizon she could see that the afternoon held an almost numinous luminescence, as an orange glow reflected off of the scintillating mirrored surface of rock solid frozen ice. She stood in amazement of how awesome Mother Nature was, and thrilled to the beauty of God's everlasting creation: boxwood plants and evergreen; *how did they withstand the bitter cold?*

Crystal, too thoroughly engrossed in her mental game of observations to notice an approaching sixteen- wheeler throttling down the slippery steep hill, suddenly snapped back to reality. She was so busy ignoring that loquacious egomaniac, puffing on his cigarette and standing too close to the edge of the sidewalk. The blaring horn of the semi approaching at breakneck speed interrupted her thoughts. It was skidding down the mountain slope dangerously and heading straight towards the two of them! The Warden pretended not to care; however Crystal fearfully took two steps back, just as a wise precaution.

Thunder…Thunder… ThunderCats…ROAR!!!

In an instant, the young Ms. Knight took courage and said a quick prayer up to the heavens, pre-soliciting God for his supernatural strength and divine mercy. Sensing an opportunity to even up the score, while avenging the suicide of her friend, Crystal took a glance around to make sure no one was watching her.

Then, just as the massive truck came careening towards the sidewalk, Crystal sucked in a deep breath and violently shoved The Warden in front of the tractor-trailer. The anxious driver anticipated the impact of the collision and mashed on the brakes to try to bring the behemoth vehicle to an abrupt stop. It was all for naught, as this maneuver caused the truck to jackknife across the center divide of the highway. It had happened so fast, right there in the blink of an eye!

Filled with a courageous spirit, as well as thankful that she remained safe during the debacle, Crystal calmly walked over to where The Warden lay in the middle of the street. His mangled body was juxtapositioned just shy of the front grill of the truck, spewing deep cerise blood all over the white snow. The driver had not yet exited the cab, so Crystal bent down to hear what the big man was saying. Gurgling noises escaped his throat, as he wailed *"Help me, help me."* Soon traffic in the opposite direction came to a complete standstill.

As Crystal confidently crushed her right sneaker firmly into his neck, thereby snuffing out his life, she yelled:

"This is for the death of Ariel Basquez, you bastard!"

When she was apprehended, yanked from the accident scene and escorted back to the confines of the facility, Crystal passed by the rushing Catholic priest and said,

"Forgive me Father, for I have sinned..."

PART FOUR

"The road to success is constantly
under construction."

Anonymous

CHAPTER 13

Detective Don Dellevega hung up the office phone, still reeling from the call that he just received from the mother of his beloved girlfriend. He came into his job to tie up some loose ends, and seek some refuge from the desperate situation he faced back at home. Crystal was still in a coma, with no signs that she was going to make any kind of recovery. Absolutely no signs whatsoever. The doctors were becoming more pessimistic by the day, and the expenses of maintaining a round-the-clock attending nurse was beginning to put a daunting drain on his cash reserves.

Still, he kept up his prayer vigil as a spiritual warrior. Tired of feeling pitiful and powerless, he was now ready to turn his pain into purpose. It was time to work; for he knew God was able to perform miracles!

At the same time Dellevega sighed because he realized that he was harboring a growing resentment towards his mate's mother, Ms. Clarissa Turner Knight. Crystal had already told him on numerous occasions about her parent's bewildering lack of support, acknowledgment, and unconditional approval. Her mother was always seeming to criticize anything she tried to accomplish. She also had a nasty habit of pitting Crystal against her brother, Mr. Rayburn Knight. Clarissa could find no fault with the younger sibling, putting him up on a pedestal, while praising everything his own family did.

Right now, Crystal really needed the positive support of all of her closest family and friends. She needed a strong network to cheer for her and root for her survival. What she *did not* need was even more drama.

Yet here was Clarissa, about to start stirring up muddy waters again. Calling to request some sort of favor, she didn't even realize that her daughter was fully incapacitated at the moment. Fighting for her life. Destiny and well-being hanging in the balance. She was always so busy asking Crystal for stuff, that it never occurred to her that the well had finally run dry.

And wasn't it all her fault, anyway?

Dellevega didn't want to nurse any grudges against the elder woman, but he secretly blamed her for the entire fiasco. Wasn't it actually *her* idea to guilt-trip Crystal into taking that expensive cruise to Singapore with her pastor's church ministry? Didn't she insist, in her best holier-than-thou attitude, that it was vitally important for Crystal to experience a once-in-a-lifetime chance to hand out gifts to the less-fortunate? Didn't she set it up to look like she would not approve if Crystal happened to refuse to give to the charity generously?

Clarissa Turner Knight had made it seem like Crystal would miss her shot at getting into heaven, if she didn't cooperate with her demands. *What a load of malarkey!* Hogwash! Dellevega wasn't sure of what went down across the seas in Singapore, but Crystal nearly ended up in heaven- and ahead of schedule! His honey nearly got herself shipped home in a body bag.

As Dellevega approached his 56th birthday, he found that his patience with people was becoming more and more limited. Other people who incessantly brought their own drama to his doorstep *got on his last nerve.*

If they were constantly begging for money…Drama!

If they complained too much about illnesses…Drama!

If they were always in a fight with someone…Drama!

If they asked for advice but never took it…Drama!

If they liked to brag alot, but never had nothing to show for their waste-of-time life on Earth… Drama!

If they tried to use words to make you feel guilty about something that had no real value at all…Drama!

If they were regularly up in your face, draining your energy and demanding your attention, but added nothing of substance to your daily existence…Drama!

If they routinely voiced their *unsolicited* opinion about things that were none of their business…Drama!

Add to that, the fact that Dellevega was acutely aware that Clarissa didn't like him, really didn't care for him at all. The first dig was when she slipped up and called him Ricki on the phone. That famously deceased actor was one of Crystal's most troubling psychotherapy clients. The kid was nearly half his age and was born in the Dominican Republic. Whereas he hailed from Puerto Rico, was a life-long dedicated public servant in law enforcement, and had been living with Crystal for a few months. *What was the mix-up?*

Crystal confessed that her mother disapproved of their relationship because he was only a few years younger than her. *Nonsense!* He knew that the feeling he had for his ladylove was genuine and true. Crystal was a rare breed, a wild bird at times; yet sweet and docile too. He hoped to bring stability and secureness to her otherwise erratic life. That girl could be in a gangland shoot-out one day, then swinging from the rafters as an acrobat the next. But she was still his precious lover!

Still, this was the bullcrap that Dellevega was currently contending with. Along with being targeted for AARP membership; staying near a bathroom due to a weak bladder; chewing softer foods because his teeth hurt; avoiding direct sunlight so he didn't get heatstroke; and showing up for annual physical exams for prostate cancer screening. Yeah, like that would be lots of fun!

Sometimes there was a small, still voice deep down inside of Dellevega that expressed that he wished he could've done it all over again. Maybe he should've pursued a more leisurely line of work: like surfing, rock-climbing, race-car driving, deep-sea diving for ancient treasures, or just traveling all around the world.

However, a leopard can't change its spots, any more than a tiger can put on new stripes. He was the same calm, peaceful, reliable, predictable, and dependable gentleman that his parents had raised him to be. He was always going to put God first in his life, and he would forever be a die-hard football fan. *Go Giants!*

Some things never change…

Dellevega's train of thought was interrupted by his supervisor, saying that he needed to see him promptly.

"Oh here we go again," Dellevega whispered under his breath. It probably had to do with the fact that he just got this post a few months ago, and went on extended leave of absence already. He knew his rights under the Family Medical Leave Act, but sometimes it just boiled down to this: *either you're on the job or not…*

CHAPTER 14

Dellevega gazed upon his younger counterpart with an air of slight suspicion. He was accustomed to decades of taking orders from the 'rank & file.' He had also been a part of the top brass, back in San Juan. Those promotions had been hard fought for, and won fairly. Yet this dude just seemed to have risen through the chain of command by some other means of ascension.

Something just didn't seem right here. Even with a double major in Computer Forensics and Cyber Security, this character just didn't fit the part. Not that Dellevega held anything against those who had the golden opportunity to attend college. He himself was born into poverty, and thus took the military/ police officer route. Now, this rookie university graduate, with little or no field experience, was running his own unit and calling all the shots? No, he still didn't quite belong in the gritty, seedy underbelly of investigations.

Dellevega was recently recruited to actively join the Anti-Human Trafficking Task Force, shortly before moving to New York City to be with Crystal. Now here he was, out on his own; first December holiday ever spent in this harsh, bitter cold. His colleagues assured him that this was one of the worst winter seasons on record, but that still made the frigid temps hard to bear. Removing his fedora, he welcomed his youthful boss,

Billy Intaglia, into his messy cubicle of a workspace. He was first and foremost, a team player.

Mr. Intaglia stepped into the crowded space and took a look around. Scribbled handwritten notes and close-up surveillance shots of various 'persons of interest' were pinned haphazardly to the dull grey cloth material. Intel about their latest criminal suspect, Mr. Juan Rosario Ortega, abound everywhere. It was like walking into a 3-D photo booth depiction of his life. His daily whereabouts were fully documented on these three flimsy little cubicle walls. It was an old-fashioned technique, yet it provided 'the big picture.'

"Hey there, Dellevega. I'm not really sure how you guys used to do things back home, you know in the dinosaur age, but we really don't use this type of methodology anymore." Billy stood there with a smug smile on his face, letting his dry sarcasm sting a little.

Dellevega wanted to wipe that silly grin off his face, but decided to play it cool. He sensed that his new supervisor had more than just a friendly visit in mind.

"Well, it may seem kinda ancient, but it gets the job done. I like to put the pieces of a puzzle together, then slowly take a step back and see the patterns emerge."

"Oh is that what they call it, huh? Trend-spotting. In the digital age, we don't leave people's confidential information laying around on display like this. Anyhow, couldn't this be better stored away in a file?" Billy swept his hands over the panorama for emphasis.

"I guess so, but that's not the purpose of your visit today, now is it? So let's skip over the housekeeping formalities. Go ahead and free your mind. Speak."

"Say, how's your pretty girlfriend? I believe Crystal is her name. How's she doing these days? Billy cast his stare down to his shoes, and shifted nervously from one foot to the other; like he was very uncomfortable.

"Oh, no change. Still in the same comatose condition."

Dellevega was slow to simmer, but could feel his blood beginning to boil. He was accustomed to dealing with these young punks with overgrown egos, and prided himself on being able to remain calm in any situation. However, there was only so much a man could take, and he knew when someone was deliberately messin' with him. *Don't lose your head...*

"Yeah, that's unfortunate. Sorry to hear that. Hey, let me get straight to the point. I have it on good authority from the higher-ups, that we're ceasing all surveillance on Mr. Ortega. So that means you can end your case."

"You mean close this file. Forever? After what he and his goons did to Crystal? Sorry *amigo*, it ain't ever gonna happen. This case is not solved until that fugitive is finally captured- that's either dead or alive."

"I'm telling you man, there's some heavy pressure coming from above that we have to cease-and-desist. His legal team of high-powered attorneys are swamping us with character defamation litigation. Unless we come up with some hard-core evidence soon, they're threatening to shut down this whole operation. Is that what you want, for good men to lose their jobs, all because of your own personal vendetta?"

Dellevega shook his head slowly, staring at Billy Intaglia intensely. Whenever he analyzed facial features that closely, he was trying to pinpoint the similarities to individuals he'd come across before. Nothing really stood out as familiar. Except the nose. Something about that nose was too unique to ignore. Somehow Dellevega had come across his tribe before, he just couldn't remember where. It was a *hook* nose.

"Hey dude, are you paying this any attention? This is a very serious matter. One of life and death. I can't stress the importance of this situation enough, or make it any clearer. You've been instructed to stand down."

"Nah, I can't do it. I just can't do that. He's too evil to let him slip through our nets once again. Someone has to stand up to these rich men with power, who bully their way through the world. Where's your sense of justice? Where's the sense of righteousness, man?"

"Look, forget righteousness. I got a mortgage to maintain. That million dollar condo in Astoria ain't gonna pay for itself. I thought you would see the wisdom of this, cooperating with the rest of the team. However, since you choose to buck the system, I must insist that you turn in your gun and shield. You've been given a direct order, and if you intend to disobey it, then you've got to hand in your letter of resignation ASAP. In addition your security clearance is revoked."

"*Ay Dios mío*! It's like *that*? You're just gonna beat a brother down like that? Snatch all his weapons, take away his reason for living? I'm a good, honest, hard-working man. I've been paying my dues in this country for the past thirty years- I don't deserve this!"

"Stand down, soldier. This isn't your fight anymore."

"Well, I may have lost this particular battle, but the war is not over. It's never over until good triumphs over evil, in the end. I will continue my combat, but just on a different field. You can't stop me, Intaglia!"

"And what about Crystal's long-term involvement? What about her other shady activities, and keeping things that don't belong to her? Like those diamonds."

"*What?*" Dellevega screamed incredulously. Now he really wanted to wring this chump's neck. "What are you talking about? Are you out of your damn mind?"

"Well, I'm just saying. Just playing devil's advocate."

"Last time I checked, Satan didn't need your help!"

"Whatever…" His ex-boss rolled his eyes, then spun around on his heels and exited the cubicle. Dellevega stood there for a moment, dazed and confused, before realizing that he had just been fired from his position.

As he began to pack all of his accumulated papers into a large cardboard box, his brain raced with random thoughts. From paying the $6000 a month rent on the mini-maisonette that he shared with Crystal, to his own personal need to keep his healthcare insurance going.

No other job contacts sprang to mind as Dellevega thought to himself,

"Now what in the heck am I gonna do?"

CHAPTER 15

In a complete haze, Dellevega stumbled back to his BMW with his brown box of belongings. Parking near the "A" train at West 4th Street in Greenwich Village, he limped over to MacDougal Street to buy himself a $3 falafel sandwich. Confident that he could kick the mental fog with a full stomach, he then looked around for a good place to sit and think for a while. Crystal had introduced him to this area when he first arrived in New York. It was her old stomping ground for many years when she attended the doctoral program at NYU.

Making his way over to Washington Square Park, he found an empty bench near the Arc de Triomphe, and plopped down for a spell. As he watched the throngs of tourists streaming by, dressed in their festive holiday gear, he began to think about his troubles less.

There were the usual assortment of ne'er-do-wells present during the middle of the day. Homeless men and heroin junkies shuffling around aimlessly, begging for change. Shiftless souls. Ghosts of their former selves, shells of the men they were always meant to be.

They reminded him of the *moko jumbies* that his mother used to tell him about when he was a little boy growing up in Puerto Rico. These creatures of Afro-Caribbean legend were zombies that roamed the earth, delighting in nothing more than dabbling in mischief.

Thinking of his mother's bedtime stories, and her delicious cultural dishes, like *platanos maduros*, made Dellevega a little homesick. Although his parents had passed away many years ago, he still reminisced on them fondly. He recalled that they gave him love, and they gave him guidance. They were very poor people, but they instilled in him a love for Father God; as well as a sense of right versus wrong. He never held their meager lifestyle against them, and cherished them always for giving him a solid foundation to build upon.

So therefore, he was *not* lazy. He was dedicated, hard-working, and committed to leaving this world a better place than how he was born into it. That's what his parents had taught him as a young man, and he always wanted to make them proud. *Tough times never last, but tough people do!* He knew that if he just kept the faith, God would come through with an amazing solution to all of his problems. He just had to wait…

Shifting the box off of his lap onto the faded wooden bench, Dellevega looked up somewhat concerned when one of the strange characters of the park ambled over towards him. The bedraggled bum held forth a fist full of large worn marble chess pieces, challenging Dellevega to a duel in exchange for a twenty dollar bill. Thinking that he couldn't lose, Dellevega agreed.

Placing the money on the table, he admitted that while he loved the game of chess, he was actually more of a *dominoes* kind of man. After all, that was more in keeping with his Cuban heritage. The indigent looked at him with a blank expression, then set up the pieces.

Needing to get a few things off his chest, Dellevega started to talk casually about the events that happened to him that day. How he was just fired by his boss; how he was newly arrived in this city; and the continued coma of his beloved girlfriend. The man listened attentively, nodding his head occasionally and asking pertinent questions. As Dellevega unloaded his conscience more, analyzing the twists and turns of his life, he became distinctly aware that he felt lost today.

His moves were usually carefully planned, and his decisions were ones that he didn't regret later on. Was it a mistake to sell his condo in San Juan and come to this fast-paced city? He felt like a fish-out-of-water.

"Tell me a little more about your girl, what's she like?" The bum seemed genuinely interested, as he pushed a rook forward to capture a pawn, leaving his queen unprotected. It was a fake-out sacrifice move.

Dellevega began to tell the tale of how they first met at the airport in Puerto Rico. She was all he could think about ever since. Somehow, he knew that his destiny was meant to be intertwined with hers. She had a funny personality and was moody sometimes, but still Crystal brought a rich new milieu to his life's tapestry.

"Sounds to me like you need to be willing to fight for your love, young man. Don't let that lady get away!"

"Yeah, I know. But like I said, she's in a coma right now, so there's really not much I can do." Dellevega shuddered at the thought of losing Crystal at this juncture. If this crisis didn't resolve itself in his favor, he wasn't sure how he'd be strong enough to carry on.

"Oh that's just her hiding in her own little fantasy world. It's all smoke and mirrors, just like *Alice* in the wonderland. Right now she's trying to recalibrate, and converse with God on an uninterrupted basis. But you, my brother, better be ready for when she wakes up. For that's when the real fun begins!" He winked slyly.

Now it was Dellevega's turn to stare blankly. How could this impoverished older gentleman know so much about his current situation? How could he speak with such knowledge and confidence when he obviously owned so little? Was it all a ruse or a good omen? Dellevega had a sixth sense about these things.

"Don't worry, be happy! God works in mysterious ways; and just when you think it's too late, *He'll* show up right on time. Hallelujah! Amen, praise to my lord."

Dellevega stared keenly down at the chess board, contemplating his next move. He was so busy listening to the man's comforting advice, that he didn't even realize that he was just a few moves away from being checkmated. He'd already lost some key pieces.

"If you're looking for someone who seems perfect, you're never going to find that. Just decide on what level of crazy you can tolerate, then team up as partners and conquer the world! Some people are a little rough around the edges, and some are smooth operators. Either which way, only rare diamonds are flawless!" The bum smiled widely, dropping a knight.

Dellevega graciously bent over to reach under the table, but couldn't find the missing piece. When he erected himself again, he found that the bum was also missing.

And so was the money...

CHAPTER 16

Dellevega sat shivering as the cold chill in the evening air signified that the winter sun had begun to set. Suddenly deciding that he was not willing to sacrifice his own queen just yet, he jumped up with renewed vigor and made his way home to Brooklyn Heights. After dumping the contents of his work box all over the kitchen counter for closer scrutiny, he fixed himself a ham & cheese sandwich, and a hot cup of mint tea. Feeling better, he headed upstairs to relieve the night nurse of her duties in caring for his woman.

With the house completely empty and quiet, Dellevega went into his personal closet and punched in the combination numbers to his gun safe. Pulling out his back-up firearm, a 9mm Glock 22 pistol that he hid for safe-keeping, he also checked to make sure that he had enough ammo. In case of an intruder, or any other unexpected showdown, he wanted to be ready to defend himself and his loved one. War was declared on this day, and he was getting ready for Armageddon!

After he was satisfied that he had enough bullets, guns, and cash money to launch an invasion into a small country, Dellevega turned around and headed over to Crystal's private closet. He found it odd that the word 'diamonds' had been mentioned twice in one long day.

And that was not a coincidence!

We all fall short of the glory of God... wasn't that what he was taught back in Sunday school? *Let he who is without sin throw the first stone...* well he hadn't led a perfectly clean life himself, but if there were indeed diamonds involved, he was gonna be throwing more than just stones. He was gonna have a fit if he found out that Crystal was lying to him, and keeping secrets. There's only so much drama that one man can take before he loses his temper over things.

Dellevega tore through the house searching for that secret stash of ice. He emptied out her shoe closet, opening up 60 clear plastic containers. He reached into all of her coat pockets. He felt along the rim of the clothes hanger bar that spanned the width. He even went through her favorite professional make-up artist case. Stumbling unexpectedly across a hidden cache of Oreo cookies made him crack a smile. Suddenly he felt ashamed of himself, and had to spend hours putting it all back together again. Crystal was a real neat freak and would kill him if she woke up to a mess.

Heading back down to the kitchen, Dellevega put on his reading glasses and began to re-construct the data.

Seeing everything spread out, with anecdotal notes scribbled underneath surveillance photos, only made one thing clear. First of all, there were no mentions of stolen diamonds anywhere in the file. Only a murky business transaction conducted in Nigeria to own a controlling interest in an old oil drilling conglomerate.

Secondly, the organ-snatching operation had appeared to go underground, with less shipments being visibly tracked out of

South America. Perhaps the Task Force had been successful in stopping the abduction of children being sold for body parts. If so, that was a huge endeavor that he was indeed proud to be a part of. Anything that would put a crimp in the style of an evil millionaire mastermind, was worth the dangerous undertaking involved. It took a lot of time and energy to coordinate that massive international joint effort.

Speaking of international, it appeared that the dirty criminals that Mr. Ortega did business dealings with, hailed from all over the world. Semiautomatic rifles from Russia, crude oil from Africa, tanks from Germany, raw cocaine from Bolivia, and sex slaves from the Philippines. Anonymous bank accounts in Switzerland and the Cayman Islands. Expensive real estate property and luxury resorts owned in Morocco, Panama, and Costa Rica. Gulfstream G650 private jet and pilot to fly around the globe on a moment's whim.

This madman had his hand in so many different pots…

The only connection that Detective Dellevega couldn't figure out, was one weird stakeout where Ortega was snapped meeting with some mob bosses. The conversation was not tape recorded, but it took place in front of a known mafia hangout with family ties that went back many generations. Now, what did he want with the Italians? Did he hope to snag a piece of the gambling, extortion and racketeering operation that they carefully built up through the years? These were not the easiest sort of people to get in bed with; once you cross them, know that it would cost you your life!

Exhausted from hunching over the kitchen counter for nearly an hour, Dellevega walked into the livingroom to sit in his favorite recliner. This was the chair that he watched football in. This was the chair he took his naps in. This was the chair he did his best thinking in.

Yet something about this mystery just didn't add up…

What did Billy the Kid know about Crystal's past, and her having "items that did not belong to her?" With all the crime going on in the world today, why was his Task Force supervisor so concerned with Crystal having some diamonds? How did he ever get recruited for that job in the first place? Was it just to gain access to Crystal? Seemed far-fetched, but Crystal recently stated that she felt like someone was looking for her.

Perplexed by the whole conundrum, Dellevega rose up from his lounge chair and slowly walked back upstairs. Realizing that he left the door to his gun safe wide open, he doubled back to his personal closet. Seeing that it wasn't nearly as neat as Crystal's, he made a mental note to straighten it up one day. She was constantly nagging him to pick up after himself, and keep his belongings in tidy order. She couldn't stand the sight of clutter, and said chaos gave her headaches.

His job used to call him all hours of the day and night, so there was never enough time to go back and fix things up the way she liked it. While hanging up some of his slacks and sports coats that had fallen to the floor, Dellevega noticed a large blue cardboard box sloppily stuffed into the back of his closet. He figured he'd maybe bought some tools at the local hardware store, and forgot to take them out of the wrapping.

Absentmindedly, he reached into the nook and pulled out the box with brightly-hued letters printed on it. Turning it on its side, he read the words "Tampax Tampons: Super, 96 Count." Realizing that it was the Costco wholesale edition for Crystal's monthly period, Dellevega rushed over to her closet to place it in there. As he hurried across the room in disgust, he clumsily tripped over a pair of his own shoes that were left lying out. Just like Crystal warned, he tumbled to the floor.

The box went flying out of his hands like a failed interception and landed a few feet away. Feeling like a big ol' buffoon and glad that nobody was watching, he got up and walked over to where the contents had spilled out. At least he didn't break his back or a hip.

"I'm getting too old for this!" He mumbled sourly.

Detective Dellevega bent over and carefully picked up a long trail of tampons, one-by-one. However, after diligently retrieving dozens of them scattered about, he happened upon a separate box that had been stuffed securely inside. Prying it loose out of curiosity, he found two small jewelry packages hidden deep within.

The first package contained a hefty solid gold necklace that appeared to be a talisman, or amulet. It resembled an item that he once saw at a crime scene that involved human sacrifices and voodoo, on a plantation back in Puerto Rico. It was beautifully sculpted, with a few expensive rubies masterfully set at the bottom of the piece. As he examined it closely, a hidden jagged prong cut one of his fingers, spurting blood onto his freshly-pressed shirt. That was an unexpected shocker.

Nevertheless, the real prize was contained in a squishy, navy blue velvet pouch. When he peeked inside, he saw a spectacular scintillation…

DIAMONDS!!!

CHAPTER 17

The cat was out of the bag now...

It was nearly midnight when Dellevega discovered the hot rocks. Walking over to the bed where Crystal lay, clutching the diamond and amulet purse, he exclaimed:

"Oh baby, what have you gotten yourself into?"

Reaching over a wounded hand to caress her face softly, Dellevega drew back in utter surprise as Crystal suddenly opened her eyes and attempted to lick up his blood! It was a full two weeks since she responded to any touch stimulus, now here she was blinking rapidly. Astonished by her effort to communicate back with him, he laid the two packages on the nightstand. He had the nearest hospital on speed dial and was prepared to rush her over there, if need be. After stepping away to clean himself up, he returned to the bedroom to find his beloved sitting straight up in bed.

Ahoy, the sleeping beauty awakes!

"W...Wa...Wa-ter...Water," she slowly tried to speak.

Crystal's voice croaked, as her parched lips struggled to emit the sound. Dellevega fetched a carafe of *agua fresca* from the refrigerator, poured out a small glass and held it to her mouth.

She drank the refreshing liquid hungrily, craving more with an unending thirst.

Never once did she focus her gaze on him, instead staring off into space vacantly. However, tears were streaming down Dellevega's face, as he silently thanked the heavens for bringing his sweetheart back to the land of the living. He knew that her recovery would progress slowly, that she would resemble a re-animated human corpse at first. But he was still grateful to see that she had arisen from infinite sleep.

Not wanting to disturb Crystal's new consciousness with deep memories from the past just yet, Dellevega quickly put the troubling items away. In a safe hiding place. Tucked back in the corner of his closet. Again.

The next couple of weeks went by in a blur with a flurry of frenzied activity. A steady stream of spiritual advisers, counselors, medical personnel, rehabilitation specialists, and speech therapists paraded through the house to assist Crystal with reaching her full potential.

A procession of milestones had already passed without much fanfare: Crystal's fortieth birthday; their first Christmas living together; Angel had her baby shower (and then a baby boy); even New Year's Eve came with no champagne consumed. Dellevega blocked out the bad news from the TV and radio to protect Crystal.

Although she wasn't out for long, what an incredibly crazy, mixed-up world this was to wake up to:

The Ebola epidemic killed thousands of West Africans.

Christians were beheaded for proclaiming their faith.

There were widespread incidences of police brutality.

Chemicals were being sprayed over organic farms.

Scientists saw the "imminent collapse" of the universe.

CAN'T WE ALL JUST GET ALONG???

***

Dellevega was on his very best behavior at first- bringing home fresh bouquets of Crystal's cherished tiger lilies, rubbing her feet with shea butter every night, and not mentioning anything that might lead to an argument. But eventually, as Crystal appeared to be coming back into normalcy, he needed to hear some answers about the ticking timebomb back in his closet.

Dellevega devised an ardent plan to gently rouse Crystal back into who she was before that deadly attack. Stating that the time had come for her to finally leave the house, he purchased two tickets to an evening concert featuring Chinese performers. He knew she held a deep appreciation for all things Asian.

Up until this point, Crystal never asked Dellevega why he wasn't leaving for work each day, like before. Until now, he refrained from bringing up anything about her past. Each person did a delicate dance to preserve the idyllic peace in the home. However, time was running out and Dellevega desperately needed for Crystal to return to her prior status as a fierce warrior.

Three months had already passed by under this truce. Now it was early Spring in the Northeast, and the cherry blossom festival was underway. Temperatures were rising, and people began to peel away layers of heavy clothing. It had been a long, hard winter to endure. Hibernation made one restless for the fun and excitement that was yet to come during sunnier days.

And so it was as Dellevega and Crystal were escorted to their front-row seats in a large auditorium with a great acoustic system. It was more of an intimate setting, not really an expansive space like at Barclays Center or Madison Square Garden. Every seat had a wonderful view of the stage. It was not overwhelming.

The audience members sat around, casually chatting and munching on goodies from the concession stand. Dellevega and Crystal sat in total silence, patiently waiting for the presentation to begin. The playbill mentioned that the show featured death-defying feats performed by THE PEKING ACROBATS, so there was a heightened level of expectation in the air. Just prior to the curtains going up, a pre-recorded announcement was played regarding turning off all cell phones and the prohibition of flash photography. Expressly for the safety of the performers. Some of the theatre-goers snickered as they listened, already planning to snap pics to post to Facebook, Instagram, and Twitter. How could a few 'selfies' hurt anyone?

The first act consisted of four attractive young females with thick wooden sticks making musical merriment. Dressed in exquisite Oriental kimonos with sparkling beads and sequins, their arms flung around at lightning speeds. The way they beat those 'thunder drums,' it was hard to see how such dainty-looking ladies could possess such amazing talent and upper-body strength.

This introduction set the tone for the night, as act after act showcased astounding forté, power, precision, and agility. There was plate spinning, vase juggling, hoop- jumping gymnastics, contortionists squeezing into uncomfortable configurations, candelabra balancing, kung fu exhibitions, Lion Dance costumery, and the infamous Human Pyramid. Each elaborate scenario was increasingly mind-boggling and spell-binding in its sheer complexity. Then there was an intermission.

Crystal sat quietly in her seat in rapt amazement of the spectacles taking place. Occasionally, Dellevega reached over to rub her shoulder and assure her that everything was okay. For the finale, an assortment of aerial acrobats scurried up long scarlet red silk scarves and bamboo poles, as high as thirty feet in the air. All without nets, harnesses, lifting mechanisms or support.

This is when Crystal's eyes finally lit up with a glimmer of recognition and recollection. She recalled how she used to climb and cling to the magenta scarves during the concert tour of that rock band, R.A.G.E (Rise Against Gravity Eternal). So she was not going to live her life in a purely vegetative state!

No, she was neither a zombie, a vampire, nor a bench-warming couch potato. She was a princess, a warrior, a fearless performer, and a finely-trained assassin! Now it was time for Crystal to get back in the game.

As it all came rushing back to her, Dellevega could see a new re-energizing life force come over his partner. Now all he had to do was find a way to harvest this emerging chi, and focus it towards fulfilling their shared agenda. It was time for both of them to get back to work. But more importantly, it was time to discuss what to do about those *precious diamonds...*

PART FIVE

"When someone shows you who they are,
believe them; the first time…"

Maya Angelou (1928- 2014)

CHAPTER 18

As the New York City temperatures began to heat up, so did the relationship of Detective Don Dellevega and Dr. Crystal Knight-Davenport. Soon things were back to normal for the two. But what could be construed as normal, when life is one big crazy roller-coaster ride? With no brakes! One morning Dellevega wanted to go run some errands, but found that Crystal went and hid all his shoes so he couldn't leave the house. Halcyon days led to passionate nights, as she had *other* plans in mind. He was exhausted- with painful hickies on his neck, as well as long red scratches on his tanned back.

He couldn't help it, the man was whipped! Whenever she was doing work around the duplex, he followed her from room to room, like a forlorn little puppy. Sometimes he needed his space to think and watch sports; but most of the time, he really enjoyed her company. They engaged in delightful conversations, and could discuss any topic under the sun for hours.

But it wasn't long before strange occurrences began to intrude on their blissful time together; such as the calls. Crystal's cell phone would ring at odd hours, then the caller would mysteriously hang up when Dellevega answered; the numbers were never visible.

One time she got up to leave the house at midnight, but could offer no explanation as to where she was going. Or who she was meeting up with. Dellevega knew that it wasn't one of her friends- the three of them rarely ever contacted her these days. He also knew that she wasn't running off to see her mother, Clarissa Turner Knight. By the third or fourth incident, he made up his mind to follow her to the next clandestine destination.

One thing about Crystal however, is that she never ever locked her phone or instituted a four-digit pass code to keep out nosy-pokers. Unlike other modern females, her phone was freely accessible to Dellevega 24 hours a day, 7 days a week. It was usually either sitting in her pocketbook, or the kitchen counter downstairs, or the bedroom nightstand upstairs. He could see that she immediately deleted any text messages that didn't come from him, so that was a dead end. He had to give her credit for being so crafty.

Yet he decided to pry a little further and start checking her emails. A small voice in him said that what he was doing was wrong, that it was an invasion of privacy. At this point, his suspicions were fully aroused and the veteran policeman in him wouldn't let it be. He had to know exactly what his beloved was up to. Especially after waking up from a coma, who could possibly be so important that she would leave their bed at night?

He knew that she was one frisky little feline. He also knew men were strongly attracted to her. Dellevega didn't usually feel insecure about his ability to keep her satisfied, but with him being unemployed currently doubts began to creep into his brain. Being with Crystal was like the 'taming of the shrew,' he knew that he couldn't really control or manipulate her mind.

She was a head-strong woman who was accustomed to doing whatever she wanted. Crystal could easily afford the expenses of her seemingly lavish lifestyle (with or without those diamonds), so it was unlikely that she was a gold-digger, just keeping him around for some money. She was a financially independent girl.

So could you really blame the man?

Then one morning, while Crystal was taking a long time in the shower, Dellevega heard her phone chirp. That meant that another email had just come in. He tried to ignore it at first, but ended up caving in to his growing curiosity. Checking the inbox, he saw that it was mostly an assortment of marketing ads, online bill payment reminders, public library requests, vacation suggestions, and magazine renewal solicitations. The usual annoying stuff. Of course, there were also numerous confirmations from Grubhub and Seamless, because she had become a food delivery addict lately.

There was one email, subject line listed in bold letters, that came from a cryptic source. Instead of the sender using an actual name or corporate emblem, it was a long serial number that appeared to be from a foreign account. He clicked on the message, and it was short:

"Crystal, I need to see you. NOW!"

Dellevega stood there disbelievingly at first, then put together a plan and immediately sprung into action. He thought about that hit song "love is a battlefield," but this was ridiculous! *Was his girl cheating on him?*

Rather than confront her directly, he grabbed a duffle bag and threw some of his detective supplies into it. After nearly three decades working in investigations, he knew exactly what he wanted to bring on a stakeout. Going through his inventory, mostly culled from law enforcement and military magazine orders, he carefully selected that day's recce requirements:

1) a non-descript baseball cap to shield his identity

2) Ray-Ban Aviator glasses with reflective lenses

3) a hoodie and pair of jeans to remain incognito

4) a pair of comfortable Nike running shoes

5) a covert listening device for eavesdropping

6) Steiner compact police binoculars for a sightline

7) laptop with high-def camera for reconnaissance

Going into his gun safe in the closet, he loaded up the Glock and inserted it into his hip holster. Just in case things got a little heavy. *Just in case.* There would be no need for a melee if she was just meeting up with the girls for a cup of tea, or Sunday brunch and mimosas.

But his heart, and more importantly his gut instinct, told him that this was no outing for a manicure and pedicure. As Crystal emerged from the master bath, freshly scrubbed up, shaved, and glowing with oil essence, Dellevega made a lame excuse about needing to hit the gym. She thought nothing of it, and wished him a good workout. As he went to plant a small kiss on her cheek, he caught a whiff of her favorite Moroccan perfume. The aphrodisiac scent. The one that he found absolutely intoxicating. *Yeah, that one!*

After saying goodbye, Detective Dellevega exited the building and made a quick left turn to walk a short distance down the block. He knew Crystal would be coming out, in all her fancy finery, in just a few short minutes. He took out his binoculars and waited patiently. Half an hour later, Crystal came out in all her glitz and glamour. Face full of makeup and long hair blowing in the wind, she turned right to walk to the corner. Then oddly enough she didn't cross the street, but entered the local luncheonette. Dellevega was surprised she didn't catch a cab to go somewhere.

CHAPTER 19

Now why would Crystal need to get all gussied up, just to go sit in the diner on the corner of Clark Street? And who would she be meeting with so close to home?

With curiosity piqued, Dellevega dipped into their usual sushi spot across the street and asked to use the men's restroom. Quickly changing into more casual attire than what he left the house in, he suited up in the hoodie, jeans, and tattered sneaker outfit. Then he inserted the listening mechanism into his right ear to amplify all conversations. Walking fifty feet to the corner, he entered into the diner through the front door.

Quietly taking a nearby seat and motioning for a waiter, he tried to attract as little attention to his presence as possible. Pulling the fitted Yankee cap securely over his forehead, he was sure that no one had recognized him when he entered the restaurant. Scanning the room, he saw Crystal giddily sipping on a strawberry milkshake and laughing riotously. With each rambunctious giggle or squeal, she flipped her long chestnut waves over her shoulder in a flirtatious gesture. Auburn highlights twinkling in the sunlight.

And just who in the heck was that sitting beside her?

Who was this jive time turkey sucker catting around town with his woman? Dellevega had never been one to fly off into a jealous rage, but this time he could feel his blood starting to boil. He was about to turn it up in this piece! But first, he wanted to hear what they were talking about so he turned up the volume on his device.

To Dellevega's surprise, they were conversing in fluent French, so he couldn't comprehend a single word of it! He knew that Crystal was well-traveled and multi-lingual, but he'd never seen her like this! The chemistry sizzling between the two indicated that they were old friends sharing a few laughs. But at the same time, dude was checking her out like a hungry man eyeballs a juicy steak! The handsome fellow looked to be about twenty years younger than Dellevega, which was already a cause for concern. As far as ethnicity, it was hard to determine his country of origin. Although he spoke with a slightly European flair, his smooth bronze skin said "Mediterranean."

He had a tight, muscular build and looked like he would be a wily opponent in a close combat situation. His piercing steel-gray eyes never left Crystal's face, until he perchance looked up and noticed that they were being studied intensely from afar. That's when Dellevega saw his opportunity. He rose swiftly, then moved in closer to their table to launch a sneak attack:

"Hey Crystal, fancy running into you here! Why don't you introduce me to your little friend." Dellevega's voice was dripping with irony, masking a veiled threat.

"Hey there! Sweetheart, allow me to introduce you to Hassan St. Baptiste. He was actually just about to leave…"

Crystal didn't skip a beat, or bat an eyelash. As both her and Hassan stood up to greet Dellevega, there wasn't a note of embarrassment or humiliation to be detected in her voice. In what could only be seen as a pre-calculated move, Dellevega raised his arm for a handshake, and inadvertently revealed his weaponry.

Hassan's eyes immediately darted to the gun, as he considered what he should do. *Was this friend or foe?* He moved forward tentatively, like he was going to shake this unannounced visitor's extended hand. What happened next could only be seen as a coincidence.

A waitress was approaching their table with a hot cup of coffee and a slice of apple pie. In Dellevega's eager attempt to block Hassan's path of egress, he violently shoved an elbow into the poor lady's ribs, causing her to drop everything. Plates, liquid, and spoons clanged noisily as they went crashing to the ground. Being a gentleman, Dellevega apologized profusely for the accident, and stooped over to assist her. When he turned back around, Hassan had run out the side exit.

Angry as a beast unleashed during a bull run in Spain, Dellevega's nostrils flared uncontrollably. Chest heaving, he decided that he'd already made enough of a scene in the restaurant. Grabbing Crystal by her collar, he yanked her out onto the street and screamed:

"Who was that young punk? And where's your little boyfriend now? Why'd he run off like that if he had nothing to hide, huh?" Dellevega glanced at the Clark St. train station directly across the street; the *hombre* had completely disappeared, making a clean getaway.

Crystal stubbornly resisted as her enraged beau dragged her unwillingly back to the apartment, a few bystanders watching nonchalantly from the sidewalk. Pushing into the building, they breezed right past the concierge and their nosy next-door neighbor, Ms. Crabtree. The elderly spinster had an inquisitive, *Miss Marple*-like nature, and knocked on their door a few times to complain about noise levels. Dellevega impatiently punched the elevator button, never once loosening his grip on Crystal, who remained taciturn.

Once behind locked doors, the fleece really hit the fan.

"Now why don't you explain yourself to me, young lady. And don't try to fool me, you filthy *mentirosa*!"

"Daddy, I was going to tell you all about it. I swear!"

"Wh-why are you all dressed up to meet this man? Does he know where we live? How long have you been seeing this guy?" Dellevega was so mad, so distraught, that he nearly started to stutter. He wanted the answers quickly, but couldn't get out the questions.

"Hey honey, I thought you said you were going to the gym today? I hope you weren't intentionally spying, sneakily following me around to wave your big pistol."

Crystal knew that she was playing with fire, but needed to stump for more time. As she coyly removed her pearl earrings, she gave him the most stunning smile. She did not, however, give him a solid answer.

Dellevega had never been involved in a domestic violence dispute, but as his face turned beet red, he realized that he was about to 'catch a case' for Crystal.

"*Chica* wipe that smirk off your face, before I slap the tastebuds outta your mouth! Either you tell me what you were doing with this fellow, or I'm packing my things and I'm leaving. Tonight!" Dellevega stomped his foot on the floor to emphasize how serious he was.

Crystal slowly stripped off her clothes until she was down to a lacy white brassière and matching g-string.

"See, what had happened was..."

CHAPTER 20

Dellevega stared dimly at the rushing currents of the East River, wondering if he should thrust himself in. Being such a good swimmer from an early age, he knew that wouldn't be the method by which to reach an unsavory end. Still, the thought of jumping came as a comfort, following such a compelling turn of events.

Walking along the muddy waters, he contemplated if he should try to repair what was broken, or move forward and pursue a new future alone. After their candid discussion, things got a little heated and Crystal threw him out of the house. Now he was staying a few blocks away at the Brooklyn Marriott Hotel on Adams.

Now why'd that woman have to be so cruel? That was the thing about Crystal, she could be so demure and sweet. Or she could be demented and sadistic. Either way, he could've smacked her up a few times, shown her who's the boss. But a woman like Crystal would only throw hot grits in his face. Or slowly poison him to death. Or simply kill him in his sleep, cut off his testicles, then make deep-fried *Criadillas* in the morning. Sometimes it was painful to love her, but he still endeavored to do so, despite all the controversies.

And wasn't it that way with all human relationships?

Each and every decision-making event is a piece that is carefully placed into a puzzle. Therefore, it stands to reason that after a while, every puzzle paints a picture that says a lot about your life. That's why it's usually better to develop an agenda, a master plan that keeps you focused on a steady path to victory. Those that just take each day as it comes, usually fall into the traps that other people set for them along the way. The master plan keeps you hard-working. The master plan will keep you honestly moving in the right direction.

But what if I've already made a mess of my life?

With no immediate career plans, and love for a woman who seemed oblivious to the deceptive wiles of another man, Dellevega felt like his situation was reflective of some sort of mid-life crisis. His days and nights seemed like one long spiral down into despair.

Then there was his role in the big fat greasy mess that Crystal kept getting herself into. Since he'd personally seen the diamonds that his ex-boss, Mr. Billy Bad-Ass, had mentioned, he was now an unwitting accomplice to a crime that took place nearly two decades ago. He took an oath to uphold the law- not assist in breaking it! Add to that her time spent at the juvenile delinquent facility. Shocking. One would've never guessed it by how elegant and refined Crystal was on a daily basis.

But the icing on the cake was the recurring nightmares, as well as the series of crimes that took place in the last six months. Exhibit A: the murder of that young NBA player. Even as she avowed to avenge her older sister's untimely death, there were several other unexplained events that suggested that she had a sick, perverse taste for slaughter. The victims were all unsuspecting men, but somehow fully deserved their brutal fates. So did that make Crystal a valid vigilante, or just a blood-thirsty female serial killer? And why is it that most of Crystal's recent lovers were soon dead?

Was this appealing psychotherapist a troubled *Black Widow*? Or was she simply dumber than a box of rocks? In all his years of analyzing major crimes and sociopathic minds, he'd never seen such a beautiful suspect, it was difficult to withstand her sexy charms.

Not wanting to be a featured guest on *America's Most Wanted* or *How to Get Away With Murder,* Dellevega vowed to get to the bottom of this mystery, solving the riddle before another surprise funeral was arranged…

HIS!

CHAPTER 21

Crystal paced over the honey-colored maple hardwood floors back and forth furiously. Although the vicious argument with Dellevega was over two days ago, she was still in a raging fit of fury. A war was brewing on the horizon, and she needed to have him as her ally, not a mere distraction. It was necessary to get him out of the house- for his own safety. Now that he heard a few of her secrets, a force would be unleashed in the universe that would put him directly in the path of evil.

Mr. Hassan St. Baptiste continued to be an invaluable resource for covert information. This time he was providing some background on the recent rash of gangland violence murders taking place in New York, Chicago, Tennessee, and Oakland. Rally the troops. *Word went out on the street:* It's about. To. Go. Down.

Crystal was preparing to put on her combat gear and go to war, moving through the streets surreptitiously. It was strictly time for shadow ops. Full Metal Jacket. Things were now on a high-level, need-to-know basis, and she was moving compact. No interruptions. No friends, no family, no nosy beau- no nonsense and no drama. She didn't need them hanging around. It was a solo quest, and she was mounting up to go duck hunting alone. Dellevega wanted to know what Crystal did all day. While he was at work, she was in training.

Crystal retrieved the A/X Armani Exchange fingerless motorcycle knuckle driving gloves for her current project. Going back into *MacGyver*-mode, she sat down at her lab table and once again began fiddling with the release mechanism that she handily inserted into the black leather sleeve. It was a hidden latch meant to activate the four 3" stainless steel razor blades upon command. Having the house all to herself meant that she was finally free to explore her creativity. People made a mistake of underestimating her abilities, but woe be unto him who stepped to her without first considering the deadly consequences!

Planning was one-third of Crystal's magic recipe for success. Preparation was another, and passion rounded out the dish. When the complete meal was served up, Crystal became a hurricane force to be reckoned with.

She was an earthquake, tornado, and tsunami- all wrapped up into one and ready to storm through any town. SO BRING IT! She feared no man, ran from no army, and was on a one woman crusade to bring down an entire empire! Waking up from that coma she felt a blood-lusty thirst, so this could only mean one thing:

The BEAST was truly back!

PART SIX

"Be sure thy sin will find thee out."

And Then There Were None

Agatha Christie (1890-1976)

CHAPTER 22

Parking her latest acquisition, a gorgeous silver luxury compact SUV, in the first available spot she saw, Crystal stepped out of her brand new GLA45 AMG and deeply breathed in the night air. Trusting that a designer Mercedes-Benz 4MATIC would still be there when she got off her shift, either showed bravado or naiveté in this neighborhood, but she didn't care. With 19" wheels, a 355 horsepower torque engine, and fuel-injection turbo boost, it was the perfect get-away car.

Along with the rest of her recently updated persona, this vehicle was indeed 'over-the-top.' Flinging her new waist-length platinum blonde hair over to one side, she made a grand entrance into the club. Her shift was about to begin, and she didn't want to be late.

Strutting vaingloriously in her gold five-inch Giuseppe Zanotti firewing heels, she was firmly back at her original fashionista status. In order to play her role to the hilt, she had to first look the part: glamour hair extensions, Hollywood-style fake eyelashes, French manicure tips, high-beam sparkle lip gloss, custom Burberry trench coat, and celebrity-inspired footwear. She removed her Dolce & Gabbana shades, dropping them carefully into her gilded Louis Vuitton handbag.

Her booking agent said that this venue wasn't as bad as it looked, and the last couple of nights were somewhat uneventful. Most of the guys kept their hands to themselves while she was on stage. The biggest nuisance were the jerks who kept asking for dates, and wouldn't take "no" for an answer. Still the bouncers were pretty decent enforcers, and she was always escorted back to her car safely at closing time.

The cash tips were great, but Crystal wasn't in it for the money. She knew that the most challenging target was a constantly fast moving target. Eventually her enemies would surface out of the woodwork to feast on what appeared to be a helpless 'damsel in distress.'

So Crystal could either sit at home and wait anxiously for them to come seek her out, or she could roam the entire tri-state area until she picked them off. One-by-one. *Ten little Indians... and then there were none.*

She chose the latter.

And now it was time to stay physically fit, listen for clues as to who was doing what, and quietly observe her surroundings to not get caught off-guard. Walking into the club was like taking a step back in time. Much hadn't changed over the seventeen years since she left exotic dancing to pursue a doctoral degree in psychology. Even though she put her past in the rear view mirror, it was now threatening to creep up on her.

"Good evening, Ms. Anoushka. Welcome back."

At least the staff at this establishment were respectful towards her. Sure the other nearly-naked girls walking around had bigger booties, and were half her age, but these men knew class and distinction when they saw it.

Besides, Crystal was a forty-year old woman who didn't look a day over twenty-eight. That's why all the younger men loved her. She had taken really good care of herself, was in the best shape of her life, and had very little body fat. Toned and muscular. The coma was like a resurrection, like pressing a reset button. That's why she came up with a fantastic alter-ego: Anoushka Santini. *Bad girl around town, looking to get down.* New identity, same old destiny.

Knowing that things get stolen in these types of places, Crystal quickly secured her belongings in one of the dressing room lockers. She learned a long time ago not to look any of the girls directly in the eye, one could never tell their mental state and interaction breeds unnecessary drama. Taking a second to touch up her makeup, she heard her name announced over the loudspeaker. Scurrying to the stage to begin her set, she adjusted a shiny belly chain around her waist.

It's showtime!

As a headliner act, Anoushka Santini was not only expected to be sensual and seductive, but also visually interesting and arousingly entertaining. During the week, it was always refreshing for the regular patrons to see a brand new face on the platform. On Friday nights, the DJ took it up a notch; blending hiphop with dancehall and some pumping house music. For the lively Latino crowd, there was plenty of reggaeton, salsa, merengue and bachata. That really set the mood.

Anoushka was not only known for her attractive outfits in neon colors, but for her flexibility in working the pole. Other dancers were good at climbing up and sliding back down with their legs spread wide open, yet Anoushka was equally acrobatic on the stage floor.

127

Her tumbling, somersaults, backwards flips, and karate kicks were a real crowd pleaser. Men and women alike were in awe of her rhythmic gymnastics routine, and showed their appreciation with tips. Nearing the end of her first twenty-minute set, she scanned the large room, feeling a presence about tonight that was different from the others. *Was that Dellevega standing quietly in the corner?* She knew it was only a matter of time before she recognized a familiar face in here.

Coming to the finale of her set, Anoushka slowly slathered baby oil all over her firm, taut body. She started with her lithe arms, then whipped her long blonde hair back and smoothed warm oil down her neck and perky breasts. Holding the audience in a trance, she finished up by rubbing her long, lean legs.

When the show was over, Anoushka expected the usual cast of characters to boldly step forth and offer to buy her a drink. However, she wasn't interested in joining any raunchy bachelor parties, industry moguls, drug dealers or horny athletes in town for the weekend.

She usually came down off the stage, then made a beeline for the dressing room. It was best to conserve her energy early in the evening, rather than try to hustle up a few extra bucks circulating with customers.

"Hey lady, can I get a private lap dance with you?"

Anoushka hated to be grabbed on, especially with such a strong grip. While indignantly snatching her arm away, she swung around, only to be confronted by Dellevega. To keep the peace, she smiled sweetly and asked if he would also like bottle service. Beckoning to a cocktail waitress to set them up in the VIP area, she gently took him by the hand and led him up the stairs to the balcony. With house music throbbing, she leaned over and loudly whispered in his ear:

"Be cool Daddy, please don't blow my cover tonight."

Crystal, still in full costume as Anoushka, straddled her thick, muscular thighs across Dellevega's lap. Sitting on top of him, face to face, she decided to perform the deluxe version. Smoothing her hair around her shoulders, she leaned all the way back until her head nearly hit the floor. Grabbing his ankles tightly to steady herself, she hitched her stiletto heels firmly over his shoulders, and behind his ears. Then she proceeded to gyrate slowly, upside-down, as the DJ blasted one of her favorite reggae songs:

I know this little girl her name is Maxine... her beauty is like a bunch of rose...Murder She Wrote, Mur-der She Wrote...na na na...

He clutched at her legs, as they swayed to the reggae beat together. Dellevega could feel himself getting more and more aroused as Lady Anoushka clenched her powerful butt muscles around his manhood. Whine. Squeeze. Grind. Tug. Release. Repeat. The rhythm was intoxicating, as they both kept up the tempo to the Caribbean music. Feeling the ultimate stimulation and knowing he couldn't resist climaxing any longer, Dellevega tapped her to stop the lap dance.

"No más mamita, no más. See you mañana, my love."

CHAPTER 23

It was a clear spring day, and Crystal finally got some sleep 'cause she didn't have to work the night before. Starring at those strip joints, as Anoushka Santini, was turning her back into a nocturnal creature and she wasn't sure how she felt about that. Deciding that it was time to treat herself to a nice shopping spree, she hopped in the Benz and tore up the highway. Enjoying the scenic view of the Hudson River, she wasn't even mad about morning traffic. With the bright sunshine luring her out of her cave, this was the kind of day to be up in the mountains. Just fresh air and tranquility.

Blasting the top hits, and bopping to the music along the way, she was definitely not in the mood to hear any depressing messages from the media. Yet, following a string of annoying commercials and a weather update, a broadcaster came on to give a round-up of the news:

Another violent shoot-out reported last night, as police are struggling to cope with the sudden increase of gang activity trending in the nation. NYPD detectives were in full body armor, as several gunmen carried dangerous semi-automatic weapons, such as AK-47s.

Crystal was driving across the George Washington Bridge when she heard the bluetooth of her phone cut off the radio. She peeked at the 7" screen on her dashboard to see who was calling to disturb her drive.

"Crystal, I haven't heard from you in a while."

"Oh hi Mom. I've been kinda busy lately, but was planning to call you back." She didn't mean to pick up.

"What's going on? Why don't you call me more often? You know if you don't have time for your family, then your family won't have time for you!"

Oh here we go again, Crystal thought wryly to herself. Mommy Dearest back in full-blown guilt-trip mode. Even a coma couldn't save her from the usual nagging.

"I got tied up a little. You do realize that I'm a grown woman with an adult type of schedule, don't you?"

"Yes, but there's twenty-four hours in a day, and it only takes fifteen minutes to call your mom. You need to keep up with our family events and happenings."

"Listen, I've been keeping up with family events for the past forty years, and it has gotten me nowhere. Who else will persist in tracking down Kim's killer?" Crystal knew the mention of her late sister's name would make Clarissa immediately change the subject.

"Speaking of persistence, Ray Ray is continuing to do well after his open-heart surgery. You should come out and visit him. Say, when was the last time you saw your niece and nephew, anyway?" Clarissa Turner Knight couldn't resist serving up a full helping of guilt. When she mentioned the kids, it was game-on.

"Mother, honestly, I have a lot on my plate right now."

"Rubbish! Just remember, you'll always be a nobody until you learn how to let go of these silly grudges and come to terms with loving your family. Satan is trying to pull this family unit apart, and I won't let him do it."

Spotting the Palisades Mall on her left-hand side, Crystal realized that it was too beautiful a day to be having this conversation. Nearing her destination, she pressed a little harder on the gas pedal, watching out for all state troopers as she went speeding up the I-87.

"By the way Crystal, where are you? It sounds like you have me on speakerphone again. I was thinking that you could swing by Staten Island and pick me up."

"Oops, there's a call on my other line, gotta go…"

Crystal could feel a class-A migraine headache coming on, so she pressed the bluetooth button on the steering wheel to disconnect the call. She didn't know why she couldn't enjoy random discussions with her mother, she only knew that talking to that woman left her sad.

But all that was behind her now, for this was Crystal's favorite road trip. Driving up into the mountains with the crisp air blowing through her hair, just made her forget about all her problems. Getting off the New York State Thruway at Exit 16, she maneuvered through the voluminous tourist traffic until turning onto Red Apple Court. She had now arrived at her go-to place for designer shopping: Woodbury Commons.

After ninety minutes of continuous driving, she had finally reached paradise. All of her favorite apparel brands grouped together in easily accessible clusters. A veritable cornucopia of steals and deals. Usually she went down to SoHo for the upscale stores, but here she could indulge her fashion fix and go for a walk.

Stretching out her arms and legs in a deep yawn, she mentally prepared herself for a marathon of browsing, in the Olympics of buying stuff. As if her master closet wasn't bursting at the seams already. She aimed to cover every square inch of this merchandising mecca.

Lengthening her stride to begin exploring the whole 150-acre complex, Crystal was not worried about any stalkers, trackers, or surveillance cameras today. First stop on tour: *Saks Fifth Avenue* and *Neiman Marcus*.

After scouring rack upon rack of junior prom dresses, she was able to snag a full-length beaded evening gown for under $50 bucks! Of course, having the VIP coupon booklet helped a lot. Then, it was a quick peek at the *Swarovski* jewelry store to pick up a 36 inch crystal necklace to go with her next Anoushka outfit.

Loving that find, she moved over to *BCBG Max Azria*. They had the most banging studded leather motorcycle jackets this season. Their miniskirts fit her slim hips perfectly, and another strappy pair of gold heels joined the goody bag. There was just so much to choose from, but she knew she had to work the collections fast. After all, it was almost time to break for lunch.

Red velvet ropes lined the outside of popular stores like *Michael Kors*, *Coach*, *Ugg Australia*, and *Kate Spade*, as dozens of tourists waited patiently to get in. No time for that! Skipping past the *Nine West Shoe Outlet*, Crystal opted to go straight for the *Bebe* shop.

They had the most amazing bodycon dresses on sale! Each one hugged her physique, giving her a renewed appreciation for having such a fantastic figure. The ribbed material clung to her curves, playing up her best assets, and making her bounce giddily in the fit room. Stocking up on as many as she could carry back to the Benz, she made a mental note to stop by one key spot.

Giorgio Armani was one of Crystal's all-time favorite couturiers. The boutique was located way over on the other side of the food court, so she always entered with a million shopping bags. Still it was a must-have in her repertoire of haute couture. From evening gowns to bespoke-tailored business suits to cashmere knit sweaters, the selection was a treasure trove of sartorial elegance and refinery. Each season, she just had to have at least one chic item to round out her wardrobe.

Usually when Crystal entered this sanctuary, there would be many more male customers walking around, especially in the designer suit section. One client in particular bore a distinguished resemblance to a *James Bond 007*-type of character. He was in the process of being custom fitted for a merino wool blazer. As the senior Italian tailor expertly stretched the tape-measure across the man's shoulders, he turned around and lifted his gaze. Crystal nearly dropped her bags to the floor, as their eyes met across the room. There, on a raised platform like a bronzed Adonis magnified in triplicate before angled mirrors, stood Mr. Hassan St. Baptiste.

"Hello beautiful! We have got to stop meeting like this..."

CHAPTER 24

"Well, hello yourself, handsome. Fancy running into you here, of all places!" Crystal didn't normally believe in coincidences. Had Hassan followed her up to Woodbury Commons, knowing that she would visit this store eventually? She was so predictable like that.

"I have a special event to attend soon, and was just picking out an ensemble. If you can hang out for a few extra minutes, we can grab a bite to eat at the café."

Crystal acquiesced and starting perusing the aisles of luxurious garments, but nothing in particular stood out. Her mind was too pre-occupied with the present situation. Did Hassan St. Baptiste track her all the way up to Harriman, New York? Why would he choose an outlet store to find clothing, when it was so out-of-the-way? And where did he live anyway? He never once invited her over to his place. Why is it that all the men in Crystal's life were either princes or pond scum? There was no middle of the road, no in-between dude.

After Hassan made his purchase, he graciously offered to carry her shopping bags over to the Applebee's restaurant for food and drink. It was also the closest eatery to where she parked her car. Settling down into a booth, Crystal impulsively ordered a glass of red wine for starters. Hassan went with a Heineken lager.

It wasn't long before they were engaged in their usual witty banter, chatting and laughing boisterously. He insisted that she have another alcoholic beverage as they waited patiently for the appetizers to come out.

"But honestly Hassan, if that's even your real name, how do you expect me to trust you, when I don't even know where you live?" Crystal felt flush from the drinks but still wanted to delve into uncharted territory.

Outwardly she appeared to be chuckling, and of good cheer. However, inwardly she was wondering what she was doing here cavorting around with this strange man. In her forty-plus years alive, Crystal learned that people rarely did things for you out of a truly altruistic nature. No, nobody was selfless like that these days.

In fact, Crystal had become a keen observer of human nature, and arrived at the foregone conclusion that when people consistently chose to hang around you, it was usually for a specific reason. Either they were drawing off your high energy level, or they craved constant attention, or they were out to obtain some of your vital resources, or they wanted to exploit your important connections, or they needed you to continue stroking their ego, or they aimed at maintaining a sexual attraction with you, or they simply had nothing else better to do at the moment and thought you would make for a lively recreation to while away some time.

Either which way, there was always a hidden agenda.

Right now, Crystal was working on her own agenda, so everyone she came across was being sized up. It was being determined whether each person would likely help or hamper her efforts to accomplish key goals in life. There was no time to waste on trivialities.

Hassan paused momentarily as the waitress laid an assortment of buffalo wings, mozzarella sticks, and loaded potato skins on the table. He waited to speak until after she refilled their water glasses, then left.

"What exactly is it that you want to know about me?"

"Tell me about your background and your childhood. Where were you raised? Who was most influential in you becoming the man that you are today? What do you do for a living, and why do you keep popping up on my radar?" The red wine was making Crystal feel woozy, but these were the questions she wanted to ask.

Hassan looked around to make sure that no one was eavesdropping on their conversation. Then he drew in a deep breath, as he tried to ascertain how safe it was.

He earnestly wanted to cooperate and fully answer Crystal's interrogation, but at the same time, she was requesting some rather critical information. At this point, the less she knew about him, the better it would be for all concerned. It's not that he considered her a threat, he just wasn't ready for his true purpose to be revealed. What if it was picked up by prying ears, and fell into enemy hands? That could hurt his own plans.

Something in her smile said that if he didn't reveal an intimate detail about himself soon, Crystal was going to bounce. Then he could possibly lose her forever…

"Right now, I live everywhere and nowhere. I'm something of a peripatetic nomad, most days I live out of an over-stuffed suitcase. Between hotel rooms and the trunk of my car, where I lay my head at night is called home. Because I travel back and forth to Morocco, Italy, and the Mediterranean a lot, it's become hard for me to maintain one steady address."

Hassan could see that he had Crystal's rapt attention, so he bravely continued to answer her many inquiries:

"I don't work a traditional nine-to-five job per se, I'm independently wealthy. I can withdraw necessary funds from my account at any member bank around the world. I get paid for certain assignments that I complete successfully, but I also multiply my money by making short-term investments. Currently I have no family or friends to speak of. My parents are presumed dead, since I haven't seen them from the age of five. One day I was playing in the courtyard and some men came and told them that I had been selected.

From that day forth, I have been trained, educated, and programmed to do the bidding of one organization. It is an underground fraternity that has existed for many generations. We can trace our roots going back five thousand years- to biblical times. We have been able to dismantle several despotic regimes and evil empires.

As I said, it is a secret society of individuals who are dedicated and committed to seeing good triumph in the world of mankind. Across each and every millenia, we have been instrumental in helping to topple tyrants, as well as bring an end to satanic attempts at widespread chaos amongst the masses. We are *The Brotherhood*."

Crystal abruptly stopped chewing her food, eyes narrowing to slits as she focused on the gravity of Hassan's preposterous answer. By all accounts, he was admitting to being an integral part of a network of spies and do-gooders who went about foiling sinister plots around the globe. *But what in the sam-blazes did that have to do with her?* Had he taken a short break from his covert activities to woo her in this twisted courtship, or was it all part of some larger master plan?

Deciding that it was now time to throw in the towel, she slowly rose from the table. Still reeling from the effects of the alcohol, Crystal announced that she had to leave, then fled the restaurant at top speed. Hassan hastily paid the bill, then quickly caught up with her.

She was loading up shopping bags into the passenger side of her SUV, when Hassan walked up to her and aggressively spun her around to face him. There was more that still needed to be said, she needed to hear it.

"Crystal, I was sent here on a mission to protect you, to watch over you. That's why you're always running into me. I never thought I would end up having feelings for someone I've been assigned to track, but with you I feel a bonding kinship. Ever since we made a physical connection on that first day at the gym…"

Hassan's voice trailed off as he pushed Crystal against the car door and leaned in heavily against her. She weakly tried to stop him, tried to push him away, but was intoxicated by the drink. Intoxicated by the moment. Surrounded by the beauty of the mountains and the setting sun, she parted her lips and welcomed his kisses. For now, nothing made sense but their lust for each other. Everything would work out fine. *Later.*

CHAPTER 25

Crystal woke up in her bed with a throbbing migraine headache the next morning. *Hellish hangover.* Plus, her brain was still buzzing with the events of the night before. Hassan was definitely pushing up, making his true intentions known. Now, Crystal had to decide whether to believe his outlandish claims, or shake him loose and move away from this drama permanently. One thing was for sure, she just didn't have the chops to be in love with two men simultaneously, once again.

As if that love triangle with her previous stalker Ricki weren't enough, here she was indulging the passions of Mr. Morocco. The man with the piercing eyes and perpetual hard-on. Perhaps it was that Crystal's first impression was the right one: he was seeking to possess her. Mind, body, and soul. Appearing out of practically nowhere, Hassan already knew a lot about her, even as he kept his own personal stats top-secret.

She didn't know if she accepted all that hullabaloo about *The Brotherhood*, yet no other explanation made sense. Crystal didn't need her head to be filled with tall tales of fantasy and regalia; and she didn't like it when people quietly sought to take over her life with a whole bunch of mind-games and mental manipulation.

Sometimes people approach you with all kinds of illusory tricks, just because they think they're smarter than you. Like you'll never catch on to the subterfuge they're *really* up to. Their entire plot to con you, scam you, stunt you- is really all a hoax. A ruse game of wily cunning, control, and deception meant to give them the upper hand in a particular situation. This way they get to achieve their goals, while all you're left with is the pang of guilt, regret, bitterness, shame and humiliation. Crystal did not have time for shenanigans.

And now the headaches were back. Her brain felt like it was pulsating up against the roof of her skull bone. It hurt too much to think, it was too painful to devise a plan. This was not where she wanted to be at this juncture in her life. She couldn't afford to have a single day where she was messed up. Not one single, precious day! The enemy was waiting to devour her, so she had to be on point every second of every hour.

She couldn't be caught napping…

Satan was out to take over her life. Take over her spirit. Take over her body. Take over her house. Take over her persona. Take over her legacy. Take over her destiny. Take over, period. In order to defeat him on a daily basis, she had to be clear-headed, thinking straight, and able to make fine decisions for her future.

Crystal couldn't afford to feel sluggish, lethargic, apathetic, disjointed or detached. She needed to be a fit, fully-functional unit; one of sound body and mind.

You can either be a whiner or a warrior, but not both!

That's why she didn't know whether to trust Hassan as her so-called guardian angel, or perceive him as a foe. He committed the primordial sin of crossing the line, and taking advantage of her while she was vulnerable.

Oh sure, it all seemed like fun and games with homeboy. Until someone gets hurt. And of course, that someone always seemed to be Crystal. Every. Single. Time. You would think she'd learn her lesson from previous escapades, but the lure of lust never got old.

She had examined all of her past relationships, flings, affairs, one-night stands, and even her failed marriage. The one truth that stood out was the fact that hot sex has never solved a damn thing. Never. It didn't solve loneliness, unhappiness, depression, or general feelings of unworthiness. It didn't pay the bills, car note, or put extraordinary amounts of money in the bank. As Crystal got older, she didn't mind the fact that men continued to be so attracted to her body. Problem was, she wanted to retire it. She wanted to get her needs met by using her intelligence and personality, not by men thinking they could get some.

However, those hungry dogs just kept on coming after her. And unlike wolves, they didn't hunt in packs. So now what kind of breed was Hassan? After tenderly cupping her chin in his hands, he all of a sudden shoved her up against that car door with such force and determination. Thrusting his tongue into her warm mouth, his hands went roaming all over her body. Rubbing, stroking, squeezing, feeling. Crystal found it hard to fight him off, nor, she quickly realized, did she really want him to stop. They were consumed by the fiery excitement of the tension brewing between them.

Had this been the old Crystal, she would have thrown open the back door to the SUV, pushed down that rear seat, and ripped her jeans off for some hot, sexy lovin'. Hassan definitely seemed like he was down for it! But cooler heads prevailed when a Japanese family of four interrupted because they needed to get into their own vehicle. So much for passion in a big mall parking lot.

Crystal's head was still spinning from the bewitching spell Hassan was weaving on her last night. He wasn't a vampire or a werewolf. He was a warlock. Before they parted, he told her a little bit more about his mission. Apparently he was after the same nemesis that she had tried, rather unsuccessfully, to take down during her trip to Singapore: Mr. Juan Rosario Ortega.

His organization had witnessed this thirty-year rise to power, and had seen enough. They wanted him to be "neutralized," by any means necessary. Even if that meant sending in operatives to go deep undercover. There existed a clandestine network of informers, intermediaries, detectives, and assassins who were willing to put their lives on the line, in the pursuit of justice. Their motto was simple: *God's Will Be Done*.

This prompted Crystal to ask about that spectacular night where she almost came to an unexpected end on the rock concert tour. She thought she had briefly seen Hassan lurking around backstage, just before the aerial acrobats were lined up on the pneumatic lift platform. At the last possible minute, just as they were to join the rock band R.A.G.E. for the closing number, the drummer's girlfriend, Katya, insisted that Crystal switch places with her. It was something that angered Crystal, but ultimately resulted in her life being spared.

Hassan confirmed that he was indeed there that evening, but upon inspecting the scarlet ropes and harnessing gear, realized that something was amiss. It was too close to showtime to reason with Crystal not to perform, so he simply suggested to Katya that she was the better acrobat to be viewed by the audience. He said that her death was regrettable, but it sealed his original suspicion: *someone was out to kill Crystal!*

Speaking of strife, Crystal was still making the rounds of the various strip clubs, but the violence in the streets was so perilous she was thinking about stopping. At a joint in the South Bronx, eight thugs rushed in and robbed everybody with guns drawn. It was like the olden days in the Wild Wild West. She was able to slip out of a back window and shimmy up a fire escape, but it was definitely a close call. The increase in gang activity made it unsafe for everyday citizens to go out alone at night. Danger lurked around every corner, and dodging bullets became a daily activity.

Becoming a stripper, for the second time in her life, seemed like a great idea at first. She thought that it would allow her to keep one finger on the pulse of society, allowing her to obtain information about all the big ballers and shot-callers. Yet, as she witnessed herself being pulled down into a pit of sin and iniquity, she realized that this was not a strictly voluntary move.

And it wasn't like she truly needed the money, already having a large goose egg to live off of for a few weeks.

Even Ms. Crabtree was wondering what she was up to. Coming home one Sunday morning at 5:30 am, doing the proverbial 'walk of shame,' the old biddy tried to corner Crystal outside of her apartment door to talk. Snooping for information, she wanted to know where Crystal was coming from at that hour, and where was Detective Dellevega, whom she hadn't seen in a while.

At the end of the day, it was a whole bunch of restless, delusional young girls baring their breasts and shaking their fat rumps. Crystal didn't belong in these dens of satanic immorality. Not the first time in her early 20's, and certainly not now. With a doctoral degree in psychology, and thousands of dollars safely tucked away in the bank, there was no logical explanation for this latest descent into madness. This profession had no redeeming qualities, no upside, and no exit strategy.

There simply was no excuse for how lost she felt at this point in her life. She was always the one who knew what she was doing, and where she was going. Now everyone was abandoning ship and vacating the premises. She looked to her left and looked to her right, only to see that she was a little light on guidance.

Wasn't that what mentors were for? To instruct you, or share a few wise words of wisdom in your time of need? After you finished jumping through everyone else's hoops (or dancing to the beat of someone else's drum) for all the early years of your life, where was your proper reward? How was it that you would benefit from giving your unquestioned cooperation?

Crystal had proffered up her love and admiration on numerous occasions throughout her life. She was not a selfish, uppity, high-minded person like others made her out to be. Sure, she had the capacity to be cold and calculating when it was called for. But she also had the charming ability to be generously warm and tender.

Maybe she was so busy having fun all these years that it seemed like she was on some extended expensive, world-class cruise. A fantastic voyage replete with 'champagne wishes and caviar dreams' on an exclusive luxury yacht. Perhaps this phase of her life felt like the party was over, leaving her to flounder in the icy sea. It was like her Cinderella fairytale had come to a midnight. The prince fled the ball, and her carriage just turned into a giant rotting putrid pumpkin.

twang on the other end. It must've been kismet, 'cause her comforting voice washed over Crystal like cooling breezes on a summer porch swing.

"Ahoy there, my friend. Long time, no see! How goes the day-to-day insanity of running a psyche ward?"

"Oh there's nothing to it, my child. After many years on this job, you come to the conclusion that all of the true crazies are still walking around on the outside!"

Crystal was pleased as punch to talk to anyone who was willing to partake of her own special brand of neurosis. Especially such a treasured and respected acquaintance. At least, that was, until the lunch came.

Deciding to skip over the cloudy part about becoming a stripper, Crystal confided in her beloved advisor about her current mental state. She clued Dr. Susanna Smith in on the latest confusing developments in her love-life; including the recent argument with Dellevega, as well as her lusty attachment to Hassan St. Baptiste. She wasn't sure if the choices she was making were advancing her cause, or sliding her back.

"*Well that dog won't hunt.* Listen to me closely, the most expensive mistake you can ever make in life is to pay attention to the wrong people! The younger fella, Mr. Hassan, sounds like he's forever going to be following his own agenda. There's no future in trying to commit to someone who ain't willing to remain loyal to you- you know you deserve much better now.

Your best bet is to try to re-kindle the flames with ol' Dellevega. Just remember that you can never tell him how to be a man, and he can't tell you what it means to be a woman. Now, if only y'all can come together to partner up in a honest, loving, and faithful relationship, then that would be a road worth pursuing further. Rarely in life does your soul-mate come across your path, but you need second chances to recognize him."

"Thank you Dr. Smith, I'll try to remember that. I'm just at a critical point in my life where there's a fork in the road, and I'm not sure about which path to take."

"Life can be an interesting journey at times, but you've got to keep a steady perspective to guide you through the ups and downs. So if you're going through Hell right now, don't stop! Don't even think about pitchin' a tent and camping out. Just keep on trucking through, 'cause there is absolutely nothing to see, do, or learn there. The next town over is rather nice, however. It's called Triumph, and it borders on a scenic route named Success. Soon you'll be on your way to a happy place known as Redemption. Overcoming obstacles can be such a hard process sometimes, but remember, you can't be a champion, if you've never been in a fight!"

"Amen! I know that's right. Turning forty doesn't have to be some sort of lonely death sentence for me."

"Correct. God is faithful and just. His mercy is never-ending, and his love for you endures no matter what you've done. Perhaps you need to make a choice to go back to an originally unconfused state of mind. Choose resolutely to forego misery and embrace mental freedom. The apostle Paul said 'I will have joy in my life, whether I abase or abound,' so it's a conscious decision that only you, as an individual, can make..."

"I appreciate the reminder. Sometimes I forget that maintaining one's unfettered balance in life can be a monumental task. Petty drama and silly temptation continues to distract me from achieving my goals."

"History has proven that a man will work for a dollar, but die for what he believes in. So never stop chasing after your dreams." Dr. Smith had a million idioms.

After a few more minutes of conversation, Crystal could hear her intercom buzzing. *Hot food!* Promising to keep in touch, she bid her counselor farewell, then raced frantically downstairs to the front door. Feeling famished, she nearly tripped and fell down the steps.

When Crystal was done eating, she went over to the sofa in the living room and turned on the television. Having gorged herself to the fullest, she needed to lie down a bit. Flipping through the channels, she found an interesting program where a Christian evangelist was narrating an inspirational tale from biblical times.

The woman with the issue of blood was healed by her faith in Jesus Christ. After bleeding non-stop for twelve years, and being declared 'unclean' and set apart from society, she heard about the healing powers of Christ. She said to herself "if I but touch the hem of his garment, I shall be made whole." After she touched him, she instantly felt healed. He turned around and said "Who touched me?" The apostles chided him softly because dozens of people in the crowd were pressing onto him. He declared that he had felt 'virtue' go out of him. Seeing that she could no longer hide before the Lord, she timidly stepped forward and threw herself to the ground. He looked upon her kindly, and simply said "Daughter, your faith has healed you. Go and be in peace." This story from the book of Mark brilliantly illustrates true faith, but let us explore the principles of this boundless belief in greater detail. Consider the following three points:

1) You need to have some faith in order to identify and enjoy the blessing of God's healing. In other words, you must say what you truly believe will happen in your life, then believe truly on what you have just said. Don't nullify your positive statements with negativity, doubt, sarcasm, cynicism or any type of self-loathing.

2) God is no respecter of persons. His blessings can make even the filthiest person clean again. You don't have to have "the faith to move mountains." Just have a little faith, as small as a grain of mustard seed, and expect great miracles to remove blockages, insurmountable obstacles, and all dysfunctional behaviors from your life. Your unshakeable faith is the weapon that you use to accomplish spiritual warfare.

3) Jesus had an endearing love for all women, even those with afflictions. He took care to publicly proclaim that she was healed, so that the rest of her family and community could no longer treat her like a sinful outcast or pariah. This seal of messianic approval permanently restored her previously tarnished reputation by removing any remaining traces of shame, humiliation, or guilt. In other words, no one could continue, from that day forth, to talk bad about her or shun her from their quarters. That's an additional blessing about receiving a divine healing: not only does it come in an instant (after many years of trials

and tribulations), but it can also remove any lingering stains or blemishes from times past. That's the glory of God's unconditional love! Once you reach out for it and receive it, you are washed clean. Virtue is restored back to you, if you will only accept it as an act of faith...

Crystal listened intently, then thanked her lucky stars to have heard such wise, uplifting words twice in one day. Deep down inside, she instinctively knew that God was trying to tell her something, she just needed to sit still and listen! Renewing her pledge to start cherishing this one-and-only precious life, she returned to the chore of packing her bags for that impromptu vacation. Stashing her prized parcel in the secret compartment of her suitcase, she was convinced that a refreshing change of scenery would indeed lead to an energizing change of mind. Now ready to embark on yet another voyage of a lifetime, Crystal once again summoned a taxi to take her immediately to JFK airport...

PART SEVEN

"Hell hath no fury like a woman scorned."

William Congreve (1670- 1729)

fifteen minutes back down the coast, and featured manicured gardens to walk through, an esteemed collection of paintings, and an on-site café.

Speaking of food, Crystal realized that she was starving and suffering from jet-lag simultaneously. Not to mention, those dainty little portions served on the airlines never seemed to hold you down for very long. With one call to room service, she had a delectable dish of fresh avocado and lobster salad delivered to her bedside, along with a cup of iced tea.

Sitting on the balcony, she was surprised to watch sea lions frolicking along the craggy shore, just a few feet away; while a few whales and dolphins made cameo appearances further off in the Pacific Ocean. It was like a dream, their presence was oddly reassuring. This scene reminded Crystal of a long-ago childhood fantasy about visiting Malibu (albeit in a convertible with Ken). Funny how a seed could be idly planted in one's heart during the early formative years, then suddenly sprout out and fully blossom later on in life!

Sitting on the balcony, sipping slowly on her iced tea, Crystal reached for a morning L.A. Times newspaper.

Hoping to check out what was happening around town for the weekend, she was surprised to come across such a melancholy headline on the front page: *"Santa Monica Murder- Heiress Found Strangled in Park."* In reading the details of the case, it appeared that the authorities interrogated a list of the woman's alleged enemies, yet were stumped as to who actually did it.

The perceived motive was obviously money, but no one knew how she was strangled in one location, then the corpse moved and left to be discovered in pristine Tongva Park on Ocean Ave. Apparently, LAPD was being overwhelmed by the increase in gang activity taking place in the nearby poorer communities. Crystal shook her head as she thought to herself: *Where was Barnaby Jones when you needed him, huh?*

Maybe there was room for another detective agency in Southern California, after all. It could be a lucrative venture with a team of private investigators that were available for hire. Crystal thought about that fateful night in the back of a limousine, on an exhaustive ride back from the Hamptons, where it was joked that she could be part of the *Dellevega & Davenport Detective Agency.* How that notion thrilled and excited her now!

Sure, chasing hardened criminals and murderers was dangerous work, but whatever else did she have to do?

Closing up the newspaper and determined to catch the last few rays of afternoon sun, Crystal slid into her flip flop sandals and headed over to the Malibu Pier to watch the surfers at their passionate best. During the five-minute walk, she marveled at the mountains that rose up along the highway, as well as the mesmerizing views from Queens Necklace down to Catalina Island.

Sitting on one of the available benches, Crystal was surrounded by seagulls, pigeons, and the occasional pelican. Although she didn't have any bread pieces to throw to them, it was still peaceful company to keep. And that set the tone for the rest of a quiet evening, spent sitting by the hotel fireplace and reflecting on life. She realized that this romantic setting would've been even better with Dellevega around, but resolved herself to get some sleep anyway. The three-hour time difference was starting to affect her inner homeostasis.

The next morning, Crystal had her driver take her up into Beverly Hills to visit *The Greystone Mansion*. As the limo trudged up Doheny Road, passing by the famed Sunset Strip, she could see the enclave of lovely celebrity homes, expensive whitewashed condominium buildings, and bougainvillea-lined sidewalks. Upon arriving at the public property, she was overtaken by the sheer enormity of the main structure and vast 18-acre grounds, everything was so neatly maintained.

Compared to the dirt and grime of New York City, words could not possibly explain how incredibly clean, serene, and bucolic this enormous estate was. Nor could the entire grounds be explored in just one day. There was just too much land to cover! From the horse stables to the multi-car garage, from the massive front lawn to the allée of cypress trees evocative of an Italian monastery, from the never-ending botanical gardens to the lily pond. Situated high atop a steep hill overlooking most of the city of Los Angeles, it was a study in isolated grandeur and the excesses of money.

The formidable Tudor-style mansion itself stood at an impressive 50,000 square feet; and also served as the site of many movie sets and expensive weddings, as well as hosting The Annual Hollywood Ball. And who among the rich patrons lucky enough to be invited to such special events could forget the vacant castle's storied past? During the 1920's Prohibition Era, it had been designed, and lavishly appointed, by an old oil- magnate for the family of his only son and heir, Ned.

As the legend goes, E. L. Doheny Sr. came under fire for making a very large cash bribe to the political campaign of an elected official, Albert Fall. The actual proceeds were delivered to its grateful recipient in a black bag by none other than the thirty-five year old son, Ned Doheny, and his childhood friend, Hugh Plunkett. The two were reportedly 'thick-as-thieves' until a federal investigation was launched to uncover the financial wrong-doing. On a late February evening in 1929, just before they were to be called to testify again in court, Hugh Plunkett is said to have shot Ned in cold-blood, then turned the pistol on himself shortly before midnight. His widow was reportedly present, and remained devastated by the tragic turn of events.

So much sadness for a family who had only recently moved into their new home four months prior- and with five young children no less! Even today, the colossal home is rumored to be haunted by old ghosts.

Crystal shuddered to think of the death and destruction that followed in the wake of these mysterious murders. Peering into a dusty window to view one of the grand ballrooms, the building seemed hollow and lifeless. There were but a few visitors on this sunny day, so the empty home magnified her own sense of loneliness.

Wanting to escape this foreboding feeling of solitude and seclusion, Crystal jumped back into the waiting limo, and asked the driver to take her down to the fun and excitement of *Santa Monica Pier*. She needed to be around a crowd of people who actually had a pulse!

CHAPTER 29

After grabbing a quick lunch of veggie burger and sweet potato fries from a nearby food truck, Crystal joined the merry mayhem happening on the Santa Monica Pier. It was positively packed! Throngs of international tourists, local thrill-seekers, and talented pan-handling performers filled the pier with a lively vibe. Crystal was eager to shake off the somber tone of the haunted mansion, so she immersed herself in the sizzling seduction of the Santa Monica beach scene.

One would never know that Tongva Park, site of that ghastly discovery earlier, was just a few blocks away. But what a wonderful walk to work off lunch! After maneuvering down a long driveway ramp to get to the main amusement park area, Crystal's eyes and ears were able to drink in the visual feast of the crowded carnival. From the big colorful Ferris Wheel to the hopeful fishermen trying to catch their next meal, it was a treat to behold this venue of family-friendly fun.

Stopping to listen to one pair of dedicated musicians rhythmically beating African conga drums, Crystal dropped a $10 bill in their hat, then started to sway back and forth. This primal music brought her face-to-face with the happier moments of her lost childhood.

Before long she was energetically answering the call of the drums by dancing. And she wasn't alone! A small circle of curious onlookers began to gather there.

That electric ring of human presence was all that it took to send Crystal into a music-induced trance. Soon a frenzy spread throughout the masses and everyone was getting down to the uplifting sounds. They danced with wild abandon and care-free, open hearts of joy…

They danced because it felt good to release their collective anxiety, fear, troubles, pains, and problems.

They danced 'til chains were broken. Until demonic strongholds disappeared and violence was unknown.

They danced to celebrate all that was good in creation.

They danced for world peace amongst diverse nations.

They danced to honor Mother Nature and Father God.

They danced to summon up the strength of mighty ancestors, who would boogy all night in the jungle.

They danced to acknowledge the struggle of those generations that came before them, and for the secured freedom of unborn babies yet to come into existence.

They knew that as long as there were African drums, there was a life-force, so they all danced a little more!

Pitched to the point of exhaustion, Crystal finally had enough. Departing from the spectacle on the pier, she woozily headed down to the sandy beach area with the intention of collecting volcanic rocks and seashells. All she could muster up the energy to do, however, was collapse onto a tribal scarf she had purchased on her last trip to Hawaii. She fell down flat on her back.

After roasting in the hot California sun, with not a cloud in the sky, Crystal propped herself up on one elbow and surveyed the ambiance around her. It was a festive atmosphere: from the adjacent aquarium, to the roller coaster ride, to the burger concession feeding hungry tourists. At this wonderful haven of recreation and entertainment, Crystal felt safe as a woman on her own. Observing the small children while they played gleefully, she took note of their activities: digging for littleneck clams, building sand castles with brightly-colored plastic buckets and shovels, burying their parents in huge mounds, and watching their footsteps disappear as the tide rolled in to rinse the shore away.

She wanted to stay there forever, but decided to grab an evening meal, along with some power-shopping, at the nearby *Third Street Promenade* mall complex. Although it was within walking distance, she texted her driver to be on standby. Strolling leisurely through the streets, Crystal was amazed by how many people were courteous and polite to her. Strangers (mostly men) smiled at her and walked over to say "hello." Definitely a new experience as compared to the grim, stoic faces displayed everywhere in New York City.

Not that she was starting any East Coast/ West Coast rivalries, but the differences were as stark as night/day.

Stepping into the immaculate merchandise mecca that is *Nordstrom*, Crystal went delirious with a 'snatch & grab' shop-til-you-drop buying spree. From beauty products to decorative hairbands, she ran around like a maniac kid in a candy store. Of course this same scene was repeated in *Bloomingdale's*, where she snagged a pair of snug-fitting designer jeans on a clearance sale.

Finishing up with the purchase of a pair of patent-leather hot pink heels, she gathered up her bags, thanked the store personnel for their help and kindness, then promptly headed over to *Tiffany & Co.* to drool over fine jewelry. Spotting a delicate little pink-and-white diamond necklace that perfectly matched her new shoes, she had to step back from the counter when told that the price-tag was $14,500. Unfortunately it was too expensive to fit into her current budget- for she had champagne tastes and beer money. Settling on a snazzy heart-shaped number from the *Elsa Peretti* collection instead, she was happy to return to the hotel.

Whew! All that shopping worked up quite an appetite, so dinner-for-one was served quietly on the balcony. As Crystal sat there watching the most mesmerizing sunset, she marveled about the complexities of life. A simple change of atmosphere was able to shake off the insipid blues of those depressing winter doldrums. But now that life seemed worth living again, why not live this kind of life-style every single day? Okay, so true, she was not born rich, her finances hinged upon a few key investments made over the past twenty years (and the inflated selling price of her previous luxury condo).

It had been so long since Crystal had allowed herself to dare to dream! She had always been such a focused person. Focusing on her education, focusing on her career, focusing on pleasing her mother or ex-husband.

Then, in the past year, she became strangely pre-occupied with seeking revenge against the man who was responsible for her sister's death. Her mind had gone askew, her spirit came under demonic possession. But was that who she really was, deep down inside? Now perhaps was the time for Crystal to make up her mind to step into a state of happiness, for once-and-for-all! It was up to her to secure a brighter future...

Waking up refreshed the next morning, it was off to her next destination: the Venice Beach & Boardwalk.

Crystal was feeling so inspired that she decided to do as the locals do- take public transportation! After walking to the bus stop, she caught the #534 from Malibu down to Santa Monica, then for a dollar, took the Big Blue bus #1 to West Washington Blvd. Along the way, she was able to view the breath-taking vistas of Pacific Coast Highway and the ocean running alongside the road. Crystal was also able to interact with some interesting characters on the bus. Everyone from surf instructors to tennis coaches to drug addicts coming out of rehab, saw fit to strike up a friendly conversation during the one hour trip. It was like she had a sign on her forehead that said *"Talk to me, I'm actually from out-of-town."* By the time she arrived at Venice Beach, she just wanted to be left alone again.

In fact, after stopping at Starbucks for an iced frappe, she pulled on her shades and strolled around incognito. Crystal was getting tired of being mistaken for Mary J. Blige, Nia Long, Angela Bassett, or Beyonce. She was not a celebrity hiding out amongst the regular folk, and she was not an East Coast ambassador sent to hear what native Angelenos really thought about New York City. Although all of the male attention was rather nice, there were limits to how civil and polite she could be. Especially when she was having headaches.

Just about fed up with the whole ordeal, Crystal walked right past the bodybuilders posing at the outdoor gym, and headed straight for the sandy beach area. She skipped over the homeless bums begging for spare change (oh yeah, they were on the bus too, with their dogs, no less). Decided not to peruse the shops, galleries, eateries, and boutiques on Abbot Kinney Road. Could care less about the lurid tattoo parlors and graffiti art installations. Really didn't want to witness the circus freak side shows. *Just wanted sand.*

CHAPTER 30

Crystal was still blissfully sun tanning on the beach two hours later, when she realized she was ravenously hungry, with nary a restaurant in sight. The distance from the shoreline to the main strip seemed so far, she didn't have the energy to get up and start searching. Although she was trying to adhere to a healthy Southern California diet, she really had a taste for a *Mississippi Mudpie Sundae*. Tofu, bean sprouts, and kale salad are great, but every once in a while people need some hot fudge in their lives! Just then, a waterside entrepreneur approached her selling fresh pineapple and mango packs. *Prayer answered!* That, with a bottle of water, was exactly what she needed.

And so it went for the rest of Crystal's stay in the city of angels. She had already seen the tourist traps of the Staples Center, L.A. LIVE!, The Grove & Farmer's Market on Fairfax, CBS Studios, the Hollywood Walk of Fame, Mann's Chinese Theatre, Rodeo Drive, The Griffith Observatory, Palisades Park on Ocean Ave., Sunset Blvd., West Hollywood, Baldwin Hills, etc. She had even thought she spotted Mariah Carey doing her own grocery shopping at the Whole Foods near Marina del Rey on Lincoln. It was impossible to see all that Los Angeles had to offer, but she was grateful for the cooperation of the people and the weather-both made her want to return again for a much longer visit.

On the last day of her west coast vacation, Crystal was packing her bags when she realized that her cell phone was ringing. Looking at the "private unlisted" number on the caller id, she guessed it could only be one person:

"Well hello, Hassan. You're just the person that I want to speak to. You see, I'll be heading in your direction shortly, and may need some assistance."

***

Crystal hated to leave the rustic, pastoral beauty of the Malibu mountains behind. Her first indication that the second leg of her journey would turn out to be much more problematic than the first, was when immigration police at *Charles de Gaulle Airport* snatched her passport away from her because they thought she was sneaking into their country. Not that it was such an insane idea to take up undocumented residence in Paris, France. The annoying part is that she stood there arguing with the authorities in fluent French, while trying to catch her connecting flight to Morocco. No amount of reasoning could convince them that they had the wrong idea. The whole fiasco did not end until Crystal pulled out her New York driver's license and an old flyer depicting her as an aerial acrobat on a tour.

Once she started cursing them out in English, they finally got her drift that she was just passing through. At once, they handed her back her new-ish looking passport (they insisted it looked fake), her NYC license, NYU alumni ID card, rock tour playbill, and bid her *adieu*. It was a close call, but she was finally able to catch her connecting flight, instead of having to pay for another ticket on Air France. *Quel scandal!!!*

The bad dream, however, seemed to continue the moment she landed and speedily came through customs at Casablanca's *Mohammed V International Airport*. The customs officials took one look at her expensive Louis Vuitton carry-on tote, then instantly started to harass Crystal for a small bribe. But she was hip to this tradition of the personnel demanding tips:

L'argent? L'argent de poche? L'argent, s'il vous plaît.

She just folded her arms, stood her ground, and gave them a blank stare like she didn't know what they were talking about. Learning from the Paris incident, she didn't speak a word of French, just kept on smiling and shaking her head. Eventually, seeing that their ruse would not work, they allowed Crystal to pass through. Tired of getting the shake-down and run-around, she grabbed her luggage and headed to the curb for a cab.

What joy it was to see Hassan waiting patiently on her!

Exhausted from her transatlantic voyage, Crystal plopped down into the old Mercedes Benz rental that he secured to show her around the city. Assuring her that she didn't need her hotel reservations anymore, he took her straight-away to a friend's *riad* in Casablanca.

After Crystal was shown to her private quarters, got settled in and tucked her belongings away, she was ready to receive an extensive tour of the grounds. What she was not ready for, however, was any more of Hassan's flirty sexual advances. The flight over there had absolutely exasperated her, and she was in no mood for impromptu marathon make-out sessions, or any other form of hanky-panky. Her excruciatingly painful migraine headaches were making a routine appearance, so she wanted to keep things strictly platonic. She made the boundaries clear, so he agreed.

Looking around at her surroundings, it finally hit her: *"Toto, I've a feeling we're not in Kansas anymore."*

It was like stepping back into the ancient times of *Arabian Nights*. She was in awe of the sheer extent to which every detail in the home was a signature piece of art in itself. Gazing up, Crystal marveled at the intricate, hand-carved lattice scroll woodwork; the original 19th century crown moldings that bordered the ceiling; and ornate inlaid chests of wood/ brass/ bone. The cozy chamber also featured 15th century pottery and ceramics, custom-made Berber rugs, ceremonial wedding bed covers, pierced copper lanterns from Islamic mosques; woven leather and palm frond sofa throws and a few North African footstools used in religious rituals. Although the adjoining bath had been completely modernized with marble and stainless steel fittings, the bright blue window shutters were in keeping with the air of antiquity that pervaded the space. It was, quite simply, the room that time forgot.

Crystal said that she was hungry, and Hassan assured her that dinner would be served within the hour in the dining room, which was across the courtyard, in what was affectionately termed as "the hightower." She remembered passing through a central courtyard that featured a large shallow pool and bubbling water fountain. She excused herself to freshen up and change out of her traveling clothes, into a comfortable dress.

The savory scent of Moroccan spices roasting in a tagine began to drift up to Crystal's bedroom window, causing her to salivate further. She put the finishing touch on her visage, donning her heavy gold amulet, then made her way over to the ground level of the old parapet. The rare, four-story tower was reminiscent of a medieval fortress; said to have served as a 'lookout point' to warn of advancing troops during war times.

Passing by the brilliantly tiled pool, bordered by acacia trees and an unrestrained bush of white roses, Crystal listened to the symphony of chirping birds (notably desert sparrows and an African crimson-winged finch).

It was such a quiet and serene place, she couldn't fathom whether there were any other diners joining them for tonight's meal. Where were the other regular inhabitants of this treasured home? Or was it being leased specifically for Crystal's stay here in Morocco?

When Crystal cautiously stepped into the crumbling plaster and cement block corner structure, Hassan was already seated at the round dining table. He took one look at her in the long, flowing white cotton sundress, worn with the gold & ruby amulet, and swooned with admiration. Her body had a luminescent glow in the flickering candlelight. However, his handsome face soon took on a sad expression, as he solemnly stated:

"Crystal, please do me the honor of joining me for dinner. Sit down, for we need to talk about something very serious, and possibly hazardous to your health..."

CHAPTER 31

"Belle femme, you're lovely, but perhaps you shouldn't have come to Morocco- your life may be in danger!"

Hassan hushed as the manservant, an elderly Tuareg with head wrapped in a traditional turban, came around with hot hand towels for cleansing. He remained silent as the servant brought out the tagine. In removing the lid, a huge puff of steam and arousing aromas escaped from the pot. Inside was a slow-roasted mix of fresh lamb meat, cumin-covered potatoes, and green olives.

Grilled pita slices were brought in on an old English serving tray, along with a ramekin of white cucumber & garden mint dipping sauce, to refresh the taste buds.

Crystal greedily scooped up the delicious meal with her fingers, nearly swallowing whole chunks of meat. This was some of the best flavors that she'd ever had. After the meal was over, the manservant appeared again to wash her fingertips, and poured her a cup of tea. Hassan motioned her towards a narrow staircase and together they ascended to the top of the parapet.

Enjoying a sprawling view of the bustling Casablanca metropolis teeming beneath them, Hassan continued with his original statement. There was so much to say.

"*Mademoiselle*, tell me your true intentions for coming to Morocco. What purpose did it serve for you to come here now?" Hassan's stare was intensely stern.

"Why, for the shopping, of course! I had hoped to nab a few colorful hand-loomed rugs and wool blankets for my current home. Not to mention slippers, a designer snakeskin bag and leather jacket by one of the craftsmen. I also wanted to get a refill of that perfume oil that I purchased on my last visit to the old medina."

"Okay, there may be time for shopping in the morning, but if anything seems suspicious, you are to leave Morocco at once! I've already made alternate travel arrangements for you to reach Spain by a ferry boat."

"So much fuss, for little ol' me?" Crystal batted her eyelashes in jest, while faking a bad Southern accent.

"This is no laughing matter. You may be caught in the crosshairs of a long-standing feud between two enemy factions: Juan Rosario Ortega's men and the Italians. My sources tell me that at this very moment, a hit man has been hired to assassinate you, and will be tracking your whereabouts to retrieve that stash of diamonds."

Crystal stared at Hassan in utter disbelief. She knew her past would one day catch up with her, but didn't know that she was entangled in a web of wicked deals.

"C'mon Crystal, don't play coy with me. Look, I realize that you don't know who to trust right now, but you're in wayyyy over your head. The diamonds that ended up in your possession nearly two decades ago were being exchanged by a crooked Nigerian who stole them from South Africa, to be exchanged for a shipment of machine guns for his rebel army. At the precise moment of the noon-day negotiations, four masked men with heavy artillery pulled up and stormed into that Paramus, New Jersey jewelry store.

Taking everyone by surprise, they were able to get the jump on the security guard. Shots were fired, and they robbed the establishment of thousands of dollars worth of cash from a safe, as well as expensive designer diamond jewelry pieces. It was probably a set-up, due to an insider tip. But what they didn't know was that that store was actually just a front for a mafia money-laundering operation. The mob bosses who owned the place vowed that they would kill anyone involved in the heist. The Nigerian is already dead; so is Matthew Cummings, and Ian Holder. That just leaves Thiery Monsanto. Everyone knows that it was you, who was sitting in the driver's seat of the getaway car, because your ex-boyfriend, Bobby Lance, snitched just before they set him on fire. The Italians won't stop this witch hunt until they get those untraceable diamonds back!"

Crystal didn't know whether to feign ignorance, or spill her guts, confessing to the whole sordid affair. She had already told Dellevega about her dirty secrets from the past. He, in turn, revealed that even his Sicilian supervisor, Billy Intaglia, knew about the icy rocks. *Was everyone on the take?* It hurt too much to think, her head spinning with the subtle nuances and sly deceptions. And what, if anything, did this have to do with her arch-nemesis, Mr. Juan Rosario Ortega?

Crystal inquired as to how Hassan knew so much info.

"It's my job to know C.D.M.I., that's critical details of mission information. It could prove fatal to go into a new assignment blindly, I must get briefed on every possible angle of the story. My very life depends on it.

As for Ortega, he's guilty of committing many evil deeds, however, this latest scheme is the worst because it will have negative ramifications for many years to come. He's like the antichrist. He profits from and delights in destroying families, communities, and rival organizations. Right now, I'm told that he's in the process of masterminding a world-wide gang war. His aim is to have every gangland truce in America broken so that he can sell and supply semiautomatic weapons to the younger generations of ethnic men in poor neighborhoods. What's worse, he's also moving in on the extortion racket that's been held by the Italians.

The mafia have made millions of dollars selling "protection" to small businesses. Now, he's trying to muscle in on their operation by hiring thugs to shoot up businesses, then demand huge sums of money to make the violence stop. That's why the mob feels that they've been double-crossed by Ortega. He's already been running illegal liquor and prostitution rings for over twenty-five years, and his organization of terror just keeps getting bigger. It's cutting into their action."

"Wow, I never imagined that a silly choice that I made in my early twenties could result in so much murder and mayhem. Tell me what to do to make things right. I want to return the diamonds to the Sicilian mafia family, but at the same time, I want to ensure that Juan Rosario Ortega gets what's coming to him in the end. I've been doing a lot of thinking lately, and I believe that I've come up with a fool-proof plan to accomplish both goals. I want to live a long, peaceful life. Help me by getting a message back to the *Brotherhood* people."

Crystal reached over and hugged Hassan real tight and close, pressing her ample breasts against his hard chest. They were both pawns in this chess game of international intrigue. But this Queen wanted to WIN!

CHAPTER 32

Crystal slept horribly the next few nights. Tossing and turning and sweating and crying. Scary nightmares terrorized her during the early morning hours. It was like every humiliating moment in her life played on a twisted continuous loop in her mind's eye. She even remembered that vision she had of her spirit lifting out of her body, and traveling over a large body of water to a distant land. It ended up somewhere in the desert before she forced herself awake. That could've possibly been a warning about her journey to Morocco.

As it stood now, she was having trouble acclimating to this strange new environment. Crystal did feel safe as long as she remained within the peaceful confines of the riad, enjoying a stroll through the cozy courtyard in the mornings. Cup of *Earl Grey* tea in hand, she could leisurely walk through the lavishly landscaped garden and lose track of time. It was easy to forget about the violent, corrupt world waiting outside the house gate.

Perhaps Hassan was right, she was in over her head. At times, being here didn't feel like part of a wonderful vacation. Instead, it felt like she was foolishly sleeping in enemy territory! One morning she woke up, yawned and stretched, taking a look around. The first thing she noticed was the long silk dress with hand-applied glass beading and embroidery. It was in ombré shades of amber and lavender. Someone had laid it gently across the foot of the bed. But that wasn't the odd thing that she noticed about the room once her eyes fully opened.

Her luggage was gone!

Screaming at the top of her lungs hysterically brought in both Hassan and the manservant, rushing towards her with a silver tray piled high with breakfast treats.

"I took the liberty of having all of your bags shipped to your home address. I hope you don't mind, Crystal."

"But why? Why not ask my permission first?"

"Because you do too much shopping. It's okay to buy a few souvenirs, but how would you struggle with all that luggage once you arrived home? Be reasonable."

"No, you be reasonable!" Crystal cried, throwing a pillow at Hassan, while spying a black currant scone.

"Crystal I would personally love it if you stayed here a long time, however things are just too dangerous right now. I need to get you back to the States. Please cooperate with me. I left your cosmetics and toiletries for you in the powder room, and gifted you this sari."

"Ok, I trust you, but no more surprises- I can't take it!"

"As you wish. Once you've risen for the day and had breakfast, we'll go over to the old medina to buy the perfume." Hassan bowed politely, then left the room.

Crystal had become such a spoiled brat lately with having room service, door-to-door food deliveries, and breakfast brought to her in bed. She happily ate the fresh-made sausage and egg omelet, finishing with buttered scones. Rolling back over in bed to digest her meal, she didn't want to get up and begin her extensive beauty routine. Yet, something ominous in Hassan's eyes said that she was, in fact, in a dire predicament.

After Crystal finally got herself together, she emerged from her bedchambers looking like the famous Queen of Sheba. Hassan showered her with compliments, as well as kisses on the forehead and cheeks. He was so glad to see her wearing the exquisite dress that he had custom-made just for her illustrious visit to Morocco.

The manservant carried the last of her possessions out to the trunk of the Mercedes, and it was off to another whirlwind day of shopping. Remembering her last trip to Casablanca, Crystal knew better than to haggle over prices with the vendors. It was against their religion to speak, or even cast eyes upon, an unmarried woman. It was expected that they would only negotiate with her male companion. Crystal was relieved to not negotiate.

As an attractive young lady walking around in a city of lusty men, it was actually quite good to have an escort. Besides, most of the vendors only spoke in the old Arabic Berber language, anyway. Their vast selection of colorful hand-turned leather jackets, shoes, and bags spoke to centuries of culture and proud craftsmanship.

Crystal was even in awe of how much the ancient Moorish and Byzantine architecture had been preserved in the local cities. Some buildings had layered terracotta tile roofs, in the traditional orange-brown color; while other homes were framed with rows of high archways. It was all in stark contrast to the cement, big box modernistic homes with clerestory windows that were all the rage among the younger generation of affluent real estate owners today. Over here, the younger people knew how to live in history.

Still most of the young boys conversed solely in fluent French, seeking to re-enforce long-held invisible ties with their European counterparts. Crystal could feel their collective eyes feasting upon her, as she moved from stall to stall in the medina. She was a foreign goddess, an unwed woman who was still of child-bearing age. It was a little unnerving being in a world that was so different, and so far away from her home.

CHAPTER 33

Albeit, what was truly disturbing, was the proliferation of people who instantly dropped to their knees to beg her for money in public. She gave the first one or two a curious look, then stepped around them on the sidewalk and kept on with her business. The rest of them she didn't even acknowledge. Ridiculous! Some of these folks were acting normal just the second before. She wasn't rich, just looked for a few tchotkas.

It did come to her attention, however, that there were two peculiar looking young men who were following her around. Although they both sported Mediterranean tans, they were definitely of European extraction. They did not speak in the common French tongue, and they both had the same aquiline nose, even looked like twins. That's what made them stand out amongst the rest of the Muslim men that crowded the streets, bistros, and bazaars. By the time Hassan took Crystal to purchase her perfume, near the king's royal palace, it was hard to ignore the fact that they were continuing to shadow her every move. She pointed this out to Hassan, who immediately made a few phone calls.

Both men appeared to be in their mid- to early twenties, of Italian descent, with neatly trimmed moustaches, and stood about six feet tall each. Their sporty outfits suggested more of a rich fisherman, mariner, sailor or yachting-type of life. Their attire consisted of skipper hats, nautical striped cotton shirts, slim-fitting cropped Dockers cargo pants, and bright green Sperry boat shoes. One of the men had on a thin sand-colored trench coat, and suspiciously kept his arms pinned to his side, perhaps to conceal a weapon.

Attempting to behave normally (she even pretended to take a selfie with her cell phone, just to capture them on camera), Hassan and Crystal made a big, splashy show of picking out the proper scent. She tried on each one patiently, on a wrist or neck pulse point. He selected the one that most resembled the fragrance that she wore the night that they met at the boot camp gym.

After making the purchase, they jumped back into the Benz and sped out of the cramped market streets. Hassan deliberately increased his speed, determined to get Crystal to safety at the ferry port. From there, she would be met in Algeciras, Spain by an operative who could secure her passage back to JFK airport in New York. All they had to do was lose the two young men who were now openly following them in a Renault car.

Knowing the maze-like streets of Morocco all too well, Hassan did his best to avoid the narrow alleyways, dead-end roads, and congested round-abouts that led to nowhere. He swerved in and out of traffic, cursing at taxi cab drivers and goat-herders alike. The two men in the Renault gave chase until it was a high-speed race to the finish. Up winding city roads and through blustery desert passages traditionally traveled by sand-faring camels, the two cars sped past shocked onlookers, catching the attention of the authorities.

Once the police joined in the action, it was a high-stakes gamble to see which car would come to an explosive crash first. Thankful to have on her seat belt, Crystal was jostled and shaken up in the car's interior- trying to hang on for dear life. Every time Hassan took a hard turn at top speed, the car nearly went up on two wheels. After a while, Crystal just shut her eyes, and sent up prayers to keep herself safe.

On and on the lightening-fast car chase continued, until Hassan and Crystal reached their destination: the Port of Tangier. Thinking that they had lost those that were in hot pursuit, they tried to calmly grab her bags and hustle her onto the ferry boat to Spain. The terminal was jammed-packed with tourists and visitors.

Boarding the boat itself involved a lot of pushing and shoving to get onto the on-ramp before the foghorn was blown and the ship departed from the dock. Relieved that she would be back in the United States in less than 24 hours, Crystal turned back to wave vigorously at Hassan, who still stood on the port pier.

"Au revoir, ma chérie!" Hassan shouted loudly as the boat pulled further away from the shore. Crystal wanted to respond with something equally endearing, however to her utmost horror, the two men that had been following them closely, suddenly appeared. One came in front of an unguarded Hassan, while the other appeared to be hugging him from behind. It wasn't until two large crimson red circles formed on his shirt that Crystal realized that he had been brutally stabbed in both the belly and the back. As the two assassins disappeared seamlessly into the unsuspecting crush of the crowd, Hassan's limp body crumpled. Falling lifelessly to the ground, he ended up rolling right off the pier and into the engulfing depths of the cold sea below. Crystal cried out, but it was already too late…

And she didn't even get a chance to say "good-bye."

PART EIGHT

"By the pricking of my thumbs,
Something wicked this way comes."

From the classic play, *Macbeth*

William Shakespeare (1564- 1616)

CHAPTER 34

Once Crystal got back home on U.S. soil, she dropped to her knees and kissed the ground out of a sense of thanks and gratitude. She loved international travel, and never considered herself to be much of a patriot, but definitely refused to take her American citizenship for granted anymore. This country had its faults and flaws, but it was the land of her birthright, and therefore held forth the best promise that the world had to offer her at this point in her life. It was all she knew.

When she stepped off the elevator on her floor, tired and shaken from her earth-shattering journeys. She saw a slew of big brown boxes arranged neatly in front of her door. She also saw her nosy next-door neighbor standing over them, trying to adjust her bifocals to see by the labels, where these packages had been posted.

"Yes, can I help you with something here? These boxes are not in your way, 'cause your apartment is on the other side of the hallway." Crystal scoffed stankily.

"Oh, I was just going to knock on your door to complain about your clock radio alarm going off every morning. I didn't realize that you were on vacation."

"Ms. Crabapple, I apologize but it's been a long trip."

"It is actually Ms. Crabtree, dear, and another thing…"

"Ms. Crabtree. Crabapple. Ms. Jumbo lump crab cake on a honey biscuit bun. I don't care what your name is. In fact, the last time I looked at my birth certificate, you were not listed on it! I've just come back from abroad, where unfortunately, I had to watch one of my best friends die before my very eyes. Now if you excuse me, I just want to unlock my door and get my behind into bed!" Crystal went into neck-snapping, hand-clapping, up-in-your-face-funky-diva mode.

Realizing that it was about to be on-and-poppin' up in here, Ms. Crabtree wisely decided to pull up the nosy, condescending attitude and mosey on down to the lift.

Pushing all of the boxes inside the house, Crystal spent several minutes opening everything and making sure that her Louis Vuitton luggage was shipped over. She also looked for all of the shopping that was done while in Santa Monica. Everything was neatly packed in styrofoam noodles, and arrived unharmed. The only pieces that went missing were: a) her gold amulet, and b) the parcel of diamonds. But she knew that Hassan had found an efficacious way to dispose of both items.

Exhausted from ripping open packages, she just wanted to rest. Before long, her phone started ringing non-stop. Somehow, the drama always came in threes!

First up was Crystal's mother, Ms. Clarissa Turner Knight, who just couldn't seem to get through two weeks without calling to dump more guilt on her child.

"Hey Crystal, I haven't heard from you lately."

"Hello mother. I was away for a few days on vacation. I went back to California, which I haven't visited in ten years. Then I headed over to Morocco for a spell."

"Cali? What on earth could you ever want over there? Did you go back to Los Angeles again? Haven't you heard the gangbanger violence is getting to be out of control? It's all over the news, you should watch TV."

"Yes mother, I know. And I've also been formulating a plan on how we can stop the influx of guns into our local communities, while giving young men something of a more positive nature to reach for. As a Christian woman, certainly you can recognize the value of social activism to effect change for the future. I'm even considering moving to L.A. to enact the first phase."

"Well you can't legislate morality. Laws are already written, but character is actually built up over time. Those father-figure gangs scoop the boys up at an early age. As for moving to L.A., whatever for? With those dreadful earthquakes? Why would you want to move away from your family support base like that?"

"Because, mother, nothing is really jumping off for me in New York. It will always hold a special place in my heart, but I can't stand any more of the cold winters."

"Well alright then, it still doesn't make sense to me." Clarissa sighed to show her disapproval, then hung up.

Crystal could hear the verbal shrug hidden in that last statement. After so many years of seeking, but not finding, her mother's love and approval, it had little to no effect on Crystal now. As far as she was concerned, her mother didn't really know the person that she had become, so she wasn't about to comprehend her choices. She was done with trying to win her mother's rubber stamp of unconditional acceptance for the paths that she pursued in life. It simply no longer mattered.

From now on, Crystal just had to live for herself. After all, her mentor, Dr. Smith had told her to stop expecting apples from a lemon tree. Once you identify someone as a lemon tree, keep expecting only lemons, and one day you'll make lemonade. If you keep putting apple pie on the menu instead, it's bound to lead to a lot of future frustration. She also told her to start pruning and tending to her own fruit tree, and to stay planted, for in due season, she would bear good fruit of her own. A fruit tree is still a fruit tree, in or out of season. *Wise advice from someone who knows.*

CHAPTER 35

That chilly phone call was followed shortly by an even frostier one from the trio of *yentas* that she used to call her best friends. Although she had known them since high school, Crystal soon found that she had lost all patience for her former associates and acquaintances.

God was trying to help her defy gravity and rise above the dirt-digging, gossip-loving magpies of her youth. The Lord was ready to grace her with an eagle eye's view of the world. She wanted to bequeath a grand legacy to future generations; a worthwhile mission to leave the planet in a better state than how she found it. She dared to dream that she could spread blessings to others along the way from her birthdate until her death. It wasn't enough to just eat, sleep, take up room on this Earth and complain about things outside of her control.

"Hey Crystal, don't be forgetting about your girls!"

Eva Morales was the first to speak. When Crystal also heard the voices of Angel Smith Fontleroy and Anne-Marie Williams, she understood that she was being included on a conference call. As always, the last one.

"Hi guys, how's everyone doing? Sorry I haven't been in touch more. I just got back from Los Angeles." She gave them a brief run-down on the deals she snagged.

The first joke was: "With you spending money like there's no tomorrow, you'll soon be changing your last name to Waters. Crystal Waters. *She homeless, she homeless!*" Eva chuckled at the club music reference.

Then Anna-Marie had to chime in with her two-cents:

"Yeah, Ms. Crystal, it'll be a shame when you have to sleep next to the bums on the train, 'cause you a bag lady. Gucci bag-lady!" This jibe also elicited laughs.

"And what ever happened to that handsome younger man that was flirting with you at the gym? You know, the one with the light eyes? I think you said that he was from the Mediterranean. I wanted to meet him, if he's still single. You should hook us up on a hot date."

It was uncharacteristic of Angel to bring up such a dreadful topic, and to make such a silly request. Especially after having just given birth less than three months ago! Choking back the tears, Crystal chose not to mention Hassan's fateful end. She was still feeling raw about the events of the past couple of days, and it showed in the sudden silence on her end of the phone.

"Well this is news to my ear! Crystal was messing around with a younger man from the Middle East? What does she think this is, *Sex and The City 2*?" Anne-Marie relished any little tidbit of a juicy scandal.

"No, you're mistaken Anne-Marie. The guy I'm talking about hails from Morocco, which is in northern Africa. The trip that the four girls took in that movie was actually to Abu Dhabi, which is near Dubai in the United Arab Emirates territory." The discussion was getting confusing and giving Crystal a fierce headache.

"Whatever. She's always fishing in the wrong waters."

"It doesn't really matter, because Crystal broke up with that detective guy. Kicked his behind right out."

"Nah, I'm still rootin' for Dellevega. That's that older guy she met back in San Juan last summer. The Puerto Rican policeman with the crazy sexy limp. Yeah, he's quite a keeper. You know I gotta vote for *mi gente*."

Angel tried to change the subject by talking about the custody battle that she was embroiled in with her dad, who was suing on the grounds of her being an unfit parent. Crystal had already heard enough, and decided to wiggle her way out of their idle chit-chat and prattle. Crystal missed the good ol' days of hanging out with her girlfriends, going to the spa for mani-pedis and things like that. However, she also saw that they were each going their separate ways in their lives. She hoped to embark on a new journey herself, so maybe it wasn't possible to take them along. Everyone who grew up with you, can't always go where you're going.

Besides, she never truly got over the feeling that one of the three was a traitor, secretly waiting to tell her every move to those that wished to hurt her most. It was still a mystery as to how Juan Rosario Ortega knew in advance that she would be vacationing in Singapore last November. He wasn't present at the banquet table when she made her big announcement, so that led Crystal to believe that someone privately fed him that information afterwards. It was a disturbing thought to realize that one of her best friends was smiling in her face, while stabbing her in the back by betraying her trust. Especially in light of what happened to Hassan.

***

The last phone call of the evening turned out to be the very first one that Crystal should've made, as soon as her plane hit the tarmac at the airport earlier that day.

"Hey Crystal, I've been doing a lot of soul-searching, and I'll be ready to come back home soon. The only thing is that I can't compete with a man who is nearly two decades younger than me." It was so good to hear Dellevega's deep Latino voice; she needed him now.

"Oh honey, Hassan is dead. He was murdered before my own eyes, and I'll be next if you don't protect me!"

"Sorry to hear that! No matter what I may have felt about him personally, he didn't deserve to die so soon. Baby, say no more. I'm on the next flight back to New York. You'll hear my key in the door before morning."

Crystal hung up the phone feeling a little better, and thankful that she never changed the locks. Then she ran herself a hot bath with lavender aromatherapy oil. Stripping down naked, she sank into the deep tub to relax her muscles and ease her mind. It had been an especially hard week to endure, but somehow she made it through. After being brave for so long, she finally allowed herself to feel vulnerable, and break down. Skipping dinner, she realized that she'd lost her appetite. The next taste in her mouth was only the one of salty tears streaming down her flushed cheeks…

CHAPTER 36

Crystal awoke the next morning to a familiar sound that she hadn't heard in a few weeks- the cacophony of clashing pots, pans, and dishes being thrown around loudly in the kitchen downstairs. She almost panicked, given the fright she recently experienced, and called the police to report an intruder. Her first reaction was to timidly yell out: *"Hello, is there anybody down there?"* This inquiry was immediately met with a text message to her cell phone: "Good Morning, Baby. Breakfast is now served, come as you are...Luv, Don."

Crystal pulled herself out of bed, threw on a silky house robe, then ran swiftly down to the kitchen. Once she set her eyes upon her beloved beau, she flung herself on him and thanked him repeatedly for being there. In turn, he told her how much he missed her for every second that they were apart. Looking at the hot steamy plate sitting on the counter, he announced that they were to dine on *huevos rancheros* this morning.

Dellevega knew exactly how Crystal was. Once she scarfed down her entire delicious meal, he patiently placed the plates in the sink. After washing the dishes and tucking away the pots and pans, he sauntered over to the living room sofa. There she was, knocked out.

She was snoring so loud, he had to turn up the volume on the TV just to watch his favorite sports channels. But he wasn't complaining. It was good to be back home, even if the unspoken truce was purely on her terms. Retrieving a blanket from the closet, he covered her up so she wouldn't catch cold in her lacy lingerie.

Surprisingly, she slept for a solid two hours in her food-induced coma of sorts. Dellevega didn't disturb her. He knew that there was a lot that they needed to catch up on, especially since they were out of contact for nearly a month. His trip to Puerto Rico helped him to gather some additional intel from his old cronies on the force. It also helped him to put some things into perspective. He was a man who usually liked when his life made sense, but all that had gone out the window.

Falling in love with Crystal had meant a sudden, unexpected change in plans, because she turned his whole world upside-down on its ear. Just when he thought he had it all figured out, had all his ducks lined up in a row, here she came with her alluring beauty, and sweet, seductive words. No one had ever made such a powerful first impression on him, or impacted his life in such a short period of time. The funny thing was, he was actively praying to God to send him a good woman like Crystal. He'd already seen a fair share of silly superficial girls who bored him to death.

Although she could be fervently independent, almost to a fault, she still needed rescuing every now and then. Hence, his speedy return back to home base. He was her knight-in-shining-armor, her prince charming, and he intended to stay to protect her until it was over.

Dellevega once read that a life lived without love was like a ship without sails. One could just aimlessly drift about on the stormy seas of discontent, with no sense of guiding direction. And that's how he felt when he was showing up for work each day, but had no one to come home to, at the end of the shift. All those hours spent doing overtime, was just a ploy to mask the loneliness that he felt in his heart. Sure, he received promotion after promotion, but at the end of the day, each incremental increase in financial abundance only resulted in additional frustration. No one to share with.

Speaking of sharing, when were they going to have some children? Dellevega had always wanted a big family, but the timing just never seemed right. His first wife died before she could conceive, and he wasted a lot of years feeling sad and heartbroken. Now that he found a woman that he would be proud to call the mother of his children, he was ready to hear the sound of little bare feet, pitter-pattering on freshly scrubbed wood floors. And he would teach them how the cook good Puerto Rican food when they grew up.

He knew that Crystal was strict about defending her right to reproductive freedom, but deep down inside, he yearned to see a little replica of himself running around. Whether it was a boy or a girl, it wouldn't matter. He would love his child, and provide for his family, just the same. He wished she could set aside her own selfish agenda and hedonistic lifestyle, long enough to hear her internal biological clock ticking.

So far Crystal showed no indication that she wanted to give birth like her best friend, Angel, just did. However, he wasn't going to give up hope. Dellevega was going to keep on trying, until she eventually gave in. He was just as determined to spawn a prodigy as he was when he rose through the ranks of the San Juan police force. In the meanwhile, he was on a crusade to make the world a safer place to live- safer for his own bloodline to enjoy a brighter world of tomorrows....

CHAPTER 37

As Dellevega stared lovingly at his muse, Crystal began to stir on the sofa. Kicking off the blanket, she violently tossed and turned, all the while talking in her sleep. He leaned in closer to see if he could decipher what she was saying, figuring she was suffering from yet another nightmare. Reaching over, he gently shook her. She awoke, startled and frightened, looking like a disheveled doll that had fallen off the shelf. Dellevega gathered her up in his arms, shushing away her fears, and reassuring her that she was safely back at home.

Crystal pushed him away sluggishly, then shyly said:

"We need to talk, but I don't know where to begin."

Dellevega moved further away on the sofa, respecting her space and listening to her words. His heart yearned to hold her in his arms, but at the same time, it was obvious that there was something that Crystal needed to get off her chest. He always wanted to be that person that she felt comfortable spilling secrets to.

"Allow me to go first this time. Sweetheart, I want to apologize for getting up and leaving you vulnerable for the past couple of weeks. I should have never left the house and removed my things from the property. From now on, I promise to stand my ground, no matter what. Whatever we go through from now on, we can solve it out together. Okay? I am not your adversary."

"Yes, I believe you, darling. And I'm sorry, too. Sorry for not trusting and having faith that our love would withstand the test of time. It's obvious that you are a man of your word, and your heart is in the right place."

"Speaking of which, how is it that Hassan died? Was he a criminal on the run? Will you tell me the details behind how it is that you were around to witness this?"

"Well, do you want me to start at the beginning?"

Crystal took in a deep breath then explained that after quitting the exotic dancer gig, she decided to book a double vacation to clear her mind. First she went to Malibu- which was balmy, calm, and peaceful. Even though there were some gangland shootings, and a heiress found dead in a L.A. park. Then Crystal explained how she flew over to Morocco, by way of Paris, and knew as soon as she got there that it was a big mistake. At this point, she could see Dellevega's eyes glazing over. As a man, he really wanted her to get straight to the point, but she was taking the scenic route. As a detective, he just wanted the core facts.

Anyway, she continued, Hassan picked her up at the airport and offered her lodging at his friend's house, so she wouldn't have to be alone in a strange hotel. After a few days, she still didn't feel right so they went shopping in the medina. That's when she saw these two Italian boys, with hook noses, following behind their every move. There was a huge car chase, with police and all, but she got to the ferry port on time. That's when the two young men appeared out of the crowd and stabbed Hassan. His corpse fell into the sea.

"Before I left, Hassan told me top-secret information regarding his involvement in *The Brotherhood*. He said that his life could be threatened if anyone found out, but since he was assigned to protect me, he thought I should know. He also convinced me to give him the diamonds and my gold amulet. But I don't think he was out to double-cross me; we actually posted the parcel off together at a trusted merchant."

"Who do you think put that hit out on him? And are you talking about the Brotherhood in Puerto Rico? Like the Latin Kings, People Nation, and Folk Nation? I just got back from there and it's a big increase in activity these days. Word on the street is that the truce is about to be broken, and they're calling for a war."

"No honey, this is an underground organization that's supposedly been around since biblical times. It's a fraternity of watchers who spy on evil empires to bring them down. It's mostly a network of religious believers who are waiting for the second coming of Christ. They try not to kill, unless it's unavoidable."

"Then the two Italian assassins were probably after the diamonds. I'm actually glad that you got rid of them. I wish you had a picture, so I could run it through the international database, might get a match. I still may be able to pull some strings, call in a favor with a pal."

"Hold on, I have a fuzzy shot of them on my camera!" Crystal pulled out her cell phone and showed it to Dellevega. He instantly saw a resemblance between the two suspects and his ex-supervisor, Billy Intaglia.

"Hey, now I see how that nose runs in the family! Let me text this picture to my contact, see if there's any connection. I told you that we make a great team together. That detective agency is starting to be more than just a dream to me, I feel like it's part of our destiny, babe. But you think that I'm talking smack."

"No *papi chulo*, I don't. As a matter of fact, I'm one step ahead of you, because I already scoped out a good mixed-use commercial space for lease on Wilshire Boulevard in Santa Monica. It would be perfect for an on-site investigations unit downstairs. It also has two apartments upstairs- one for us, one for rental income."

"Now that's my girl! An entrepreneurial venture for the two of us, with a revenue-generating property, and all in a warm weather environment. No more winters!"

Dellevega couldn't hold back any longer. He'd been wanting to make love to Crystal ever since that stimulating lap dance in the strip club. Moving in a little closer to get a kiss, he was surprised when she once again thwarted his advances, pushing him away.

"Nuh uh, oh no you don't. The next time I lie down with you, Big Poppa, it won't be as your live-in girlfriend. It will only be as your new wife!" Crystal gave Dellevega a sly look and a wink, then scurried off upstairs to jump into the shower. *Leaving him to think.*

CHAPTER 38

Spring has always held a reputation for being a time of rebirth and renewal. Even the trees were finally beginning to show fresh green buds on the ends of their barren branches. Now Crystal was ready for a rebirth in her own life. It was the end of April, about to be the month of May, and she consistently looked forward to the little birds chirping outside her window every morning. As the saying goes, those birds were singing, not because they had an answer, but because they still had a song to sing. That gave Crystal hope for the future, realizing that she was not done just yet.

Many had tried to beat her down physically, or tear her down emotionally. Tried to deposit the hex of fear, chaos, and confusion in her spirit. However, God still woke her up each day, therefore this meant that He wasn't through with her yet. Despite what her wicked ex-husband had to say many years ago, Crystal wasn't giving up on the Lord, because the Lord, sho 'nuff, wasn't giving up on her! As long as she was still breathing, there was bound to be some fight left in her bones. People could count her out, if they wanted to.

It had been a cold, brutal, harsh, desperate winter but somehow sistah girl made it on through! Now that she had weathered the storms of the past calendar year, it was time to reap a harvest at the end of her tumultuous four seasons. Winter, spring, summer, fall: God was there and made provisions for it all! Hallelujah! Amen.

To that end, Crystal knew exactly the five things that she wanted in a tax-paying, God-fearing, law-abiding man: Decisiveness, Strength, Consistency, Resilience, and Discipline (self-control). Before she got married again, she was absolutely determined to not settle for anything less than the very best. This time around it would be much better. This time around, she had even more positive qualities to offer her prospective mate. But first she had to make sure that *he's the right one.*

Crystal had kissed many a frog in her lifetime, so if some man was presenting himself as a prince, she just had to make sure that it wouldn't be another mistake.

Dellevega wrote a simple letter asking Crystal to marry him, then left it on her pillow to find in the morning. In it, he selected a few verses from the biblical book of Proverbs 31: 10-31 to outline what he was looking for in his search for the perfect bride:

"Who can find a virtuous woman? For her price is far above rubies,

The heart of her husband doth safely trust in her, so that he shall have no need of spoil. She will do him good and not evil all the days of her life.

She seeketh wool, and flax, and worketh willingly with her hands. She is like the merchants' ships; she bringeth her food from afar.

She riseth also while it is yet night, and giveth meat to her household, and a portion to her maidens. She considereth a field, and buyeth it: with the fruit of her hands she planteth a vineyard.

She girdeth her loins with strength, and strengtheneth her arms.

She perceiveth that her merchandise is good; her candle goeth not out by night. She layeth her hands to the spindle, and her hands hold the distaff.

She stretcheth out her hand to the poor; yea, she reacheth forth her hands to the needy.

She is not afraid of the snow for her household; for all her household are clothed with scarlet.

She maketh herself coverings of tapestry; her clothing is silk and purple.

Her husband is known in the gates, when he sitteth among the elders of the land. She maketh fine linen, and selleth it; and delivereth girdles unto the merchant.

Strength and honour are her clothing; and she shall rejoice in time to come.

She openeth her mouth with wisdom; and in her tongue is the law of kindness.

She looketh well to the ways of her household, and eateth not the bread of idleness.

Her children arise up, and call her blessed; her husband also, and he praiseth her.

Many daughters have done virtuously, but thou excellest them all.

Favour is deceitful, and beauty is vain; but a woman that feareth the Lord, she shall be praised. Give her of the fruit of her hands; and let her own works praise her in the gates."

Upon reading such a simple and straightforward letter, Crystal's heart swelled with affection for Dellevega. Water came to her eyes at the thought of his unending devotion, loyal commitment, and unconditional love. Everyone deserves a second chance in life. Filled with such strong emotion, and choking back the tears, all she could do was utter one simple word to his proposal of marriage:

"YES!"

CHAPTER 39

It was the first game of the subway series: Yankees vs. The Mets, at the house that Ruth built. Well, sort of. The new and improved Yankee Stadium was open for business and the excitement was palpable and genuine. Derek Jeter had already retired after a long and well-recognized career, but there were still popular superstar pitchers to quote stats about and collect glossy trading cards for. America's favorite pastime was alive and well. A new generation of eager boys and girls could eat pretzels and hotdogs with their daddies while shivering as the temps dipped after 3pm.

Opening day of the new season was like a birthright, even with the $11 beers in commemorative cups. Plus it was always cool to take home a souvenir helmet, mini-bat, or any other team merchandise from the concession stands. It had become a pricey sport to fully enjoy, but that didn't stop the thousands of fans from showing up, loyally giving their love and support. All of the die-hard fans went to the balcony, while the rich yuppies streamed into the season-ticket holder and VIP seats below, right behind A-Rod. While there, they were spoiled with special perks like waiters that took their food orders in-seat. No more getting up and spilling half your popcorn while trying to shimmy past the thirteen other people in your row.

Crystal remembered those days fondly, as she placed an order for crispy chicken tenders. She knew this area of the South Bronx well, for she used to live on Walton Avenue and 163rd Street for two years. One block away from that lovely-tree lined boulevard known as the Grand Concourse. The surrounding buildings were all built like huge brick fortresses, and held the largest, most spacious apartments in the city.

Memories abounded of walking over Macombs Dam Bridge alone to get into upper Harlem to attend a house party. Crystal remembered playing, lounging, and working out in the grassy green area parks, even as a young adult. She never felt threatened or at-risk in this neighborhood. Living near the "4" train stop at 161st Street was thought to be the utmost in convenient commutes, it was a very reliable line that ran all night.

Also, the county jails were located right up the block, so the main thoroughfare was usually swarming with cops and court officers. It just felt safe to walk around during the day, especially by the McDonalds on the corner. At night the junkies used to emerge to roam the streets, so single ladies coming down the long train steps were best to shake a tail-feather, and walk twice as fast to rush on back home. The other side of Yankee Stadium was usually deserted. A few sports bars opened sporadically during games, but the rest of the streets were sparsely populated. Even during broad daylight the alleys by the parking lot were desolate. It used to give Crystal a creepy feeling to walk through there on her way home, but sometimes it was unavoidable. After all, the fastest way between two points was a straight line. Walking alone under the elevated train tracks was a test in bravery and courage.

But nowadays, Crystal had the benzie and Dellevega had the beamer. They both had wisely selected luxury vehicles to purchase, as rewards for their hard work and financial savvy. Although they could've taken the "4" train from downtown Brooklyn, Crystal reminded Dellevega that the mobs would be drunk at high noon.

But, wasn't it true though? Seeing all the attendees who ditched the car headache and rode public transportation made one's head swoon. About 40% of the frisky loud young men and ditzy blondes were completely inebriated before they even stumbled off the subway. Even if they did look cute in their blue & white pinstripe Yankees attire. Who wanted to deal with the insanity of that crazy crush hour? Even the local residents avoided eye contact with the revelers.

Sitting in direct exposure to the freezing cold was no fun either, but Dellevega had surprisingly bought tickets for the two of them, claiming that he always wanted to go there since he was a kid. Crystal obliged begrudgingly, knowing what an enthusiastic sports fan he was. As she looked around at the happy crowd filling the stadium, bright floodlights came on to illuminate the field and images flashed rapidly across the bright behemoth Jumbotron screen. Pop music filled the air through large speakers, adding to the feeling that something thrilling was about to happen.

Crystal did, however, start to warm up a little when the organ player rallied the crowd with her favorite mini-anthem: Clap. Clap. Clap-Clap-Clap. *"Let's go Yankees!"* This cry usually whipped the masses up into a wild frenzy. That, and doing The Wave. Of course, you had to watch the giant screen to know when to stand up at just the right time to wave your arms up in the air. Still, it was good to get that stretch.

It was around the 7th inning, with the score being 4-3 Yankees, that Crystal lost all patience. Although the bases were loaded and the next batter was about to walk, she was ready to go. She didn't have the steady endurance to stay awake any longer. She was just about to start nodding off, when some announcements started playing vividly on the Jumbotron. Dellevega quickly nudged her, pointing enthusiastically to the massive TV screen. There, in front of thousands of cheering fans, were the following words displayed:

CRYSTAL, MY LOVE, WILL YOU MARRY ME?

CHAPTER 40

Feeling quite verklempt and overcome with emotion, Crystal watched as Dellevega attempted to get down on one knee in the narrow aisle. Bringing out a breathtakingly beautiful two carat pink-and-white diamond ring, he waited anxiously for an answer to his proposal. Crystal hugged and kissed him for such an audacious public proclamation of his love for her. This, in turn, drove the crowd even more berzerk as their embrace was captured on the 101 by 59 foot-long TV screen. There was nothing like springtime love, and nobody needed an excuse to drink and celebrate.

Soon afterwards, the newly-engaged couple exited the stadium, amidst loud cheers of *"congratulations!"* and *"hey you guys, good luck to ya..."*

"Are you excited to become the new Mrs. Dellevega?"

"Yeah, but only if you're going to be my Knight in shining armor!" Crystal chuckled at the play on her own last name. She had no intentions on changing it.

"Well, allow me to bring your chariot around, milady."

Nightfall was fast approaching on an already cloudy, overcast day. Crystal pulled out a pair of fingerless black leather driving gloves from her purse and slipped them on over her brand-new, left-hand embellishment. Looking up and down deserted River Avenue, it was hard to imagine that thousands of people were cheering on their favorite hometown baseball team, just a few short blocks from where she was. They could've stayed and rooted the Yankees on to victory, but she was steady shivering from the evening chills.

Dellevega left her alone momentarily, standing on a dark and lonely street corner while he went to fetch the car. And they say *"chivalry is dead."* Perhaps it wasn't the best idea, especially in this neighborhood- with bling-bling adorning her fingers and everyone else still inside the stadium watching the three-hour game. It wasn't long before Crystal felt like *she* was being watched. It was an eerie, paranoid feeling that started at the nape of her neck, and soon crept down her spine into a full-blown panic. And why didn't she leave her expensive Louis Vuitton bag at home today?

Three suspicious-looking Latino males in dark hoodies came up behind her and started to speak in Spanish.

Crystal immediately pulled out her cell phone to send an emergency text message to Dellevega: "DANGER, HURRY UP!" The next thing she knew, one of the men boldly stepped forward and smacked the cell phone out of her hand, then he pulled out a small handgun and pointed it to her face. Yanking the hoodie off, his true facial identity was finally being revealed.

Thiery Monsanto stood there before Crystal for the second terrible time in under a year, making menacing gestures. Threatening to get revenge for his fallen homies, he teased and taunted her, daring Crystal to call for help. At that very moment, a navy blue BMW pulled up with police lights flashing. Dellevega jumped out so fast, the trio barely had time to turn around and react. Glock already in hand, he bust off two shots at the other assailants with uncanny aim.

Crystal used the distraction to drop her bag to the ground, close to her cell phone. With lightning fast precision, she activated the release mechanism on her custom-rigged gloves. Four shiny stainless steel blades instantly flung out, forming a deadly fist of fury. Thiery turned around and started busting off shots at Dellevega in retaliation for his boys. Timing was crucial, one of those bullets was bound to connect.

"Dirty pig! All you cops gonna get your wings."

Crystal ran up behind the distracted Mr. Monsanto, yanked him by the hair so his neck was fully exposed, then violently slashed his throat with the razor-sharp extended blades. As his cronies lay bleeding on the ground from gunshot wounds, she quickly severed his larynx voice box, windpipe, and internal jugular vein.

The whole kill scene took mere seconds to execute, it was the *Bonnie & Clyde* re-mix, Bronx gangland style.

Retrieving her belongings quietly, Crystal then ripped off the leather gloves and hopped into the waiting car. Together, Dellevega and Davenport sped off towards the nearest highway.

Disappearing without a trace...

PART NINE

You never can tell how close you are,
it may be near when it seems afar.
So stick to the fight when you're hardest hit,
it's when things seem the worst that you mustn't quit!"

Edgar Albert Guest (1881-1959)

"Really, Mother? That's funny, because whenever you tell me this, I show up faithfully and get ignored every single time. I never leave these family events feeling venerated or celebrated, merely tolerated. I hate going to a function and everyone acts like they've got better things to do, than sit down and have a conversation with me. Like I'm not good enough to be around them, or something. It's become a waste of my time."

"Oh nonsense, dear. That's all in your imagination."

"Is it? Then why don't we ever have a party to commemorate one of *my* achievements? Like when I officially became a licensed psychotherapist. And tell me again why you didn't bother coming to my college graduation. I think you said you didn't want to take the day off from work. Come now, turnabout is fair play, so stop guilt-tripping me about attending events."

"But this is important, your brother is holding a fundraiser today because his health insurance plan did not cover all of the medical expenses from his open heart surgery. He really needs your help and support."

"How much is the bill, mom?"

"About $60,000…"

"Mother, you do realize that I'm in the middle of planning a wedding, right? If anything, I should be the one passing the hat around to gather collections. I am not rich, and neither is Dellevega. We're trying to plan a truly elegant wedding, and so far nobody is cooperating. Have you forgotten that you requested that we change the date, just so you'll be on vacation?"

"Well, I didn't want to be tired after work, so I just thought it would be better if you switched the wedding date from June 15th to August 29th. That way, I can enjoy my summer vacation without any interference."

"Mother, you are impossible! Your excuses and divisive tactics are draining, so I've got to do what is best for me now. May God have mercy on your soul."

Crystal hung up the phone in a huff. Dellevega, knowing all too well the effect that Clarissa Turner Knight had on her daughter, moved over to comfort and caress her. But the damage was done. Crystal was already in tears, crying over a parent that simply refused to love her for who she was or *even tried to be.*

CHAPTER 42

"Honey, it's okay. Don't let the stress of things get to you. Tell me what you really want and we'll do that."

Dellevega could see that Crystal was beginning to buckle under the strain of making all of the wedding arrangements. Each day brought decision after decision, choice after choice. In the end, was it even worth it? Here she was trying to craft the perfect day to impress a bunch of people who cared nothing about her. She was simply an afterthought in their lives, and she knew it! Her friends from high school, her work colleagues, her extended family in far away places- none of them took the time to solidify connections or make meaningful contact with her. It was all just a ploy to dig up more gossip in her scandal-ridden life.

These were the same people who had a whole lot to say about her behind her back, then turned up their noses whenever she came to greet them with a smile.

At this point, Dellevega was ready to just elope. He wanted his bride-to-be to feel loved, happy, safe, and at peace. He wanted her to know the joy she had brought into his life, ever since that first day they met. He never wanted her to feel sad, rejected, or defeated.

But first, she had to be clear about what she wanted.

"I've always had a saying that whatever Crystal wants, Crystal gets; but the older I become, the more I see that the world actually does not revolve around me. So I learned how to compromise. Yet, I feel I've been accommodating other people's desires my whole life."

"Okay, that may be so, but today is a fresh new day."

"That's true, and now it's my time to shine. I'm so used to being controlled or manipulated, that it's a new feeling to be able to exercise my freedom of choice."

"Then tell me about your five-year plan, I know you like to think ahead a lot, but I wonder where I fit in."

"I have a secret dream that I've been nursing for the past year. It seems a little outrageous, so I've kept it to myself. Actually, I'd like to open an academy in L.A. It would be this huge, commercial loft space that has a very welcoming vibe to it: you know- youthful, but clean and structured. On one side of the building, I would host classes where I teach young ladies dance, gymnastics, aerial acrobatics, and mixed martial arts."

"Sounds good, but what happens on the other side?"

"Actually, that's where I see you teaching boys about military ops, investigations, and law enforcement."

"Use my natural talent? Brilliant!" Dellevega beamed.

"Yeah, it could even be like a certificate program so that these young men learn a trade, and enter a new career they never even considered before. There could also be an internship with Homeland Security, so they have increased opportunities when they graduate. It's all about fostering literacy, discipline, self-esteem, and leadership. They need a rite-of-passage before they try to become grown men. We've got to offer them a positive, uplifting alternative to being in a street gang."

"Now that's what I'm talking about! You're such a determined woman, I know your dream will come true. I have no doubts about it, and will assist in the set-up."

"Thanks babe. I realize that it sounds like one of those 'super-save-a-ho' schemes, but it's really important to me that we leave a legacy behind. Today's young folk need to feel special and valued, just like what Ms. Ligurio did for me back at the juvenile delinquent facility- it made all the difference! Working with the next generation is one way to make a lasting impact."

"I agree. Now what do you want for this wedding?"

"To be totally honest, I'd like to just cancel all of this nonsense and go get married on the beaches of Hawaii. That's where I feel most at ease, and I'd love to share that experience with you. Not just on a honeymoon, but for the nuptials, as well. We could just go alone."

"That's more my style. Besides, since I got the boot from my ex-supervisor on the task force, I don't know if I trust my colleagues enough to invite them to a wedding; I think a private affair is the best way to go."

"I hear that, I never did find out who was leaking all of my personal information to my enemies last year. Speaking of your crooked boss, any word on the identity of those two thugs that killed Hassan? I sure would like to see them brought to justice- even if I have to hunt them down to do the dirty deed myself."

"Whoa, slow down sistah! You were pretty handy with that *Wolverine*-type contraption that nearly beheaded that punk Thiery Monsanto. I was very much impressed, and even NYPD thought that was a gang-sanctioned hit. However, these two professional assassins are a completely different story. Your pal, St. Baptiste, must've been in way over his head, 'cause they have a reputation for being the best in the business. They supposedly only get called when their family wants to send a prime message to their enemies.

The brothers' names are Scopetti and Cardone. You were supremely lucky to have escaped an encounter with them, alive and unharmed. Reportedly, they were found as orphans and brought up by a rich, but vicious, crime syndicate family. They are known as the 'waste management team' because they clean up problems and make them disappear. These are dangerous men!"

"Actually, I don't think it was luck. Before we left the medina, I devised a plot to take the heat off of me with regards to those damn diamonds. A few calls were made to spread the word, and a message was transmitted to the right people. I can't fathom why Hassan had to die…maybe he just knew too much."

"Exactly. I suspect that my ex-boss, Billy Intaglia is somehow related to Scopetti and Cardone- the resemblance is striking. That's probably why our targets keep shutting down their operations and skipping town, just as we move in for the sting. You'd be surprised how many men in law enforcement are making extra money by being on someone's payroll."

"It wouldn't surprise me at all. I have a degree in human psychology, remember? Sometimes you have to put yourself in the mind of a psychopath, in order to catch a killer." Crystal waited for a response to that last statement but Dellevega just stood there staring back at her silently. The truth of the matter was this: he was proud to know that his lover wasn't too afraid to ever have his back in a brawl. However, her scary behind didn't learn nothing about abnormal psyche in no stinking textbook. This chick was crazy for real!

Having caught a glimpse of her multiple personalities, he already considered her to be something of a maniac man-eater, or sadistic vampire-slayer. No one creeps up behind a guy and slits his throat- nearly decapitating homeboy, then goes shoe shopping the next morning for a wedding! Although Crystal could not face the truth about who she really was (that was part of her *scotoma*, or emotional blindspot), he knew an assassin when he saw one, and just prayed that he never pissed her off enough to turn her against him.

Dellevega was smart enough to have already made an appointment for them to attend some pre-marital counseling with a Catholic priest. Before he could walk down the aisle and say the words "I do," he first needed to know that Crystal was de-programmed from her bloodthirsty agenda, or at least had an *exorcism of her inner demons* to be able to lead a normal life!

CHAPTER 43

In a last minute bid to be selected as the 'Maid of Honor', each of Crystal's three friends made an attempt to bribe their way into the wedding party. However, despite their competitive nature, there was sufficient reason not to bestow that title upon any of them. Crystal still had her doubts as to their intentions.

Although it seemed petty to pit each friend against the other, she was starting to feel like she didn't want to have any bridesmaids at all. It was just too complex getting the three girls to agree on the appropriate attire.

Angel categorically insisted that she should be the maid of honor, yet refused to even consider making Crystal the godmother of her newborn baby. She didn't even invite Crystal to her son's christening ceremony! Eva was far too tall in the heels that she planned on wearing. The shoes elevated her height to 6'1", putting her on par with the groom! Anne-Marie, who was steadily gaining more weight, went on ahead and had her own dress custom-made without Crystal's permission. As if this move wasn't presumptuous enough, the fabric was in a yucky yellow color that was not in keeping with the overall color scheme of the wedding. It was as if they were secretly trying to sabotage Crystal's vision of perfect wedding photos.

The whole situation was so stressful, she couldn't even concentrate as she went into 'downward-facing dog' position on her rubber mat. Thinking that some yoga meditation would be a good break and release the excess tension, Crystal invited her three friends to an introductory class of Bikram yoga. However, this plan for soothing relief soon backfired, as their pervasive foolishness began to heat her up even more than the hot lava stones in the sauna room. So much for zen…

For approximately an hour and a half, Crystal ignored her three girlfriends on purpose, but they still managed to get on her nerves anyway. Eva ended up getting into a fight with the yoga instructor (who turned out to be something of a drill sergeant with a nasty mouth), and cursed her out in Spanish in front of the whole class. Angel, who had put a deep conditioning mask in her hair, took nearly 40 minutes to rinse it out in the shower. There was a small mutiny, as the other women waited impatiently for their turn in the stall. And not to be outdone, as soon as the four girls left the detoxifying yoga class, Anne-Marie dragged everyone to a bar around the corner to have drinks. Crystal instead threw up her fingers, and quipped: *"DEUCES, I'm out!"* She was fed up with the madness, and just wanted to head home to Brooklyn Heights, and the serene confines of her Clark Street duplex apartment.

***

"He said WHAT?" Crystal screamed incredulously.

She was just discussing with Dellevega how it seemed odd that the save-the-date cards went out over a month ago, and none of her family members had bothered to RSVP, as requested. The printing and assembly of the official invitations was going to be very expensive, and they didn't want to order too many of them if people couldn't make the wedding ceremony on the pre-selected date. It was a matter of a courtesy response.

After caving in to her mother's demands to move the whole affair to August instead of June, it was crucial that people let their availability be known. Especially before the final deposit was left on the catering hall for the reception. Crystal was planning to throw a huge, blow-out affair but didn't want to walk into a room full of empty chairs, if this could be avoided. She decided to call up a few folks to see why they were stalling on confirming their attendance on the biggest day of her life. She did realize that this was her second marriage.

Not having much luck, she rang up her eighty-year old Aunt Minnie, who finally told her the truth. Her brother, Mr. Rayburn Knight, had secretly made a pact with everyone at his barbeque last month, that they were not to attend Crystal's wedding because she didn't contribute to his medical expenses fundraiser. He reasoned that if she didn't want to be around family when she was invited, then everyone should boycott her invitation, and not bother to attend her functions.

Crystal's head went reeling when she heard this. Her own brother sought to destroy her special day and sabotage her wedding plans! It was no wonder why everyone she contacted gave her the cold shoulder! He never once had the decency to call her up himself to complain or air out his grievances. Instead, he was being sneaky and subversive by always hiding behind their mother to do his dirty work. Crystal hung up the phone, not knowing what to say, but definitely feeling some kind of way. *Why did her family hate her so much?* This just confirmed her deepest fears about the dismissive vibes that she always got at those reunions.

She was screaming at the top of her lungs when Dellevega came home from shopping for a tuxedo. He heard her yelling from the elevator, and came bursting through the door like the building was on fire. Having witnessed her talking to herself on previous occasions, he gently inquired as to whom was she talking to now. Crystal was hysterical, but calmed down enough to explain the situation with her family's lack of interest.

"Great, then it's agreed. We call the whole shindig off, disown your side of the family, and elope to L.A. without sending out an address-update to anyone!"

Dellevega's wry sense of humor was not a comfort at this moment when Crystal was so emotionally high-strung, so he did the next best thing. Gathering her up in his arms for a giant bear-hug, he offered to whip up her favorite Cuban sandwich with some of the left-over *pernil* from last night. Panini press, pickles, and all. Knowing that the way to Crystal's heart was through her stomach, he was not surprised when her face lit up, and she immediately dropped her hissy fit.

CHAPTER 44

After Crystal had eaten until her belly was full, and she fell out in the usual spot on the living room sofa, Dellevega gingerly brought up his plans for the next day: "Uh honey, I made an appointment for us to go to pre-marital counseling tomorrow. It had to be early in the morning. I'll set an alarm so we're not both late."

"Counseling, for what? You're doing just fine, and I'm hanging in there. Holding my own, keeping it real. Are you afraid that our marriage will end in divorce?"

"No dear, it's not that. It's just something that I was raised with as a child. This is what I need to feel whole again. Just do it for me, I'd appreciate it. OK?"

"Alright honey, if it makes you feel better, then it's not too much to ask. But who are we going to see? I'm a psychotherapist, so I already know what will be said."

"Don't be such a smart aleck!" Dellevega rolled his eyes and went upstairs to set his clothes aside. This was the only time slot that he could get for their session, and he didn't want to be dragging his feet in the morning. Crystal was sure to be grumpy without any breakfast. She wasn't a true early-riser anymore, as evidenced by her moody attitude the next morning.

Sitting in one of the back administrative offices of a nearby church cathedral, Crystal sipped on her Iced Venti Mochaccino, thinking that the cups were never big enough to satiate her thirst. She liked a lot of milk and sugar in her coffee, and there was always too much ice in the cup for the baristas to get it just right.

"Crystal, you remember Father Fulligan from the banquet last November, don't you? He agreed to meet with us before starting his daily rounds. We're lucky."

She smiled to show her appreciation, then quickly went back to sipping on her iced confection. How lucky was she to be out of her bed, dressed, and ready to discuss important personal matters at 7 am on a Saturday morning? She'd rather be sleeping in late!

The two men exchanged pleasantries about the weather and sports stats. Crystal remained silent until they were ready to get down to business. She was only there to keep the peace in the house and make her man happy.

Clearing his throat, Dellevega decided to take the lead. "Father Fulligan, you already know that we highly respect your advice and opinion. You also know that we are here today because we're in the process of getting married, and need a few wise words to guide us into holy matrimony. We would like your blessings."

"The best advice that I can give any couple seeking to make their union official, is to keep God as the third strand in your relationship at all times. Braid in His love and principles for righteous living into the fold, and let his guidance strengthen you in times of discord. The enemy will often come to you in different forms, seeking to destroy what the two of you have built. We saw this happen in the Garden of Eden with Adam and Eve and it still continues to plague our families today."

Crystal spoke up, filling the priest in on her checkered past and how she felt like she was carrying the weight of the world on her shoulders. Family drama, good friends lost along the way, and hearing the sad stories on the news made her even more depressed. It was becoming increasingly hard to keep her spirits lifted.

"Ask God to mold you like a piece of clay. Pray for the Holy Spirit to come into your body, mind, and soul to touch you, just one more time. This is a healing and cleansing touch, one that releases you from worrying about things that you cannot control. After all, you were created in God's image, a creation that He was supremely proud of from the start. All of your suffering has a meaning, and after a while it will all start to make sense. Everything in life has a purpose, don't ever forget that! Just as light banishes the dark, wisdom and spiritual revelation gets rid of ignorance."

"But how do you keep that in mind when you feel the best things in life have been snatched away from you?"

"Be refreshed by the renewal of your mind. This is most important, in order to delete the pain of past hurts. When your mind is pre-occupied with toxic poison, it stops you from being the very best person that you can be. Therefore, you have to work hard to maintain your peace of mind and a positive nature."

"And me, Father? What is your suggestion for a man who is trying to love a woman that is struggling with so many emotional issues? It is cowardly for a man to release the love of a woman, all while knowing that he has no intentions of sticking around to indulge it." Dellevega pledged that he was in this for the long haul.

"Keep your own spirit strongly rooted in faith. There is a saying that a woman should be so deep into God, that a man has to seek the Divine, just to find her. A man who is secure in himself is less likely to dump his mate. He won't 'cut & run' when the going gets tough, because he is confident in the choices that he's made. Men who thank God daily for their blessings will be appreciative of their partner, and are more likely to stay the course. However, insecure men always despise their intimate relationships, and seek to keep searching for another. Remember, it is virtually impossible to find a soulmate, if you don't first find your own soul!"

"Thank you, Father. Those are indeed wise words to live by. And what do you think about my beloved's campaign of revenge against the man that killed Kim?"

"But why do you continue to harbor rage in your spirit, my child? The holy word says that *anger resteth in the busom of fools.*" Father Fulligan reached for a bible.

"That may be so, Father, but in this world you're either on the side of good or evil. Nowadays, you can't stand in the middle of the road, that's how you get run over."

"Crystal, anger clouds your judgment and preoccupies your mind. This blocks God's ability to send and receive messages from you with clarity. What happens is that you get even more frustrated because you think He is ignoring your pleas. You foolishly lament why you're not hearing from Him anymore, when in fact, He's been trying to communicate with you all along."

"That makes sense!" Dellevega had a real epiphany.

"There are severe costs, penalties, and consequences for everything we do that's outside the will of God. Even though He provides us with grace and mercy, we must still realize a sense of personal responsibility. We must ultimately know the difference between right and wrong. As for your vow of vengeance, Crystal, enough blood has already been shed. Jesus died on the cross for the redemption of our sins. His flesh is the only sacrificial lamb that was ever needed. No other offering could ever trump this one selfless act in the eyes of the Lord. So repent; return to a life of giving."

"Speaking of giving. Honey, why don't we give the devil a nervous breakdown and pay off my brother's medical expenses? I know it's a lot of money, but I'm prepared to do it, if this meets with your approval."

"Okay, but only if we get to skip all the headaches of planning this complicated wedding. I've had just about all I can take of this stressful nonsense. Can we agree to stop the unnecessary drama with your family and friends? Let's start off on a harmonious note."

"Agreed!" Crystal blushed blissfully and reached over to hug Dellevega, nearly spilling the remnants of her giant cup of iced coffee. They both thanked Father Fulligan for his time, and promised to keep in touch. Once they walked out of the church, into the glowing sunshine of the Saturday morning, they both breathed in the air of new beginnings. Everyone deserves a second chance, but when you see the opportunity to start over again, you've got to grasp it with both hands.

The good thing about Detective Dellevega and Dr. Davenport was that they were passionately united in a sense of purpose. They both aspired to make a profound contribution to society. They both wanted to help other people live richer, more fulfilling lives realizing their own potential in this universe of abundance and creativity. Chasing bad guys wasn't enough; they dreamed of someday doing something meaningful with the gifts that had been given to them.

Who, therefore, would've ever thought that just like in those childhood fairytales, that it was still possible for this enchanted couple to find their *happily ever after...*

CHAPTER 45

Midway through the wedding planning fiasco, Crystal made a critical decision. She was now kicking back into 'Zen Warrior' mode. This meant that she was not going to be given over to bouts of depression, anxiety, or any more prolonged periods of debilitating stress. Nor would she allow herself to indulge in any more unnecessary worry about meaningless wedding details.

She was letting go of the reins, ditching her propensity for neurosis, and leaving her 'control-freak' ways behind permanently. No more *type A* personality. She would become a bastion of hope, peace, calm, positivity, and humility. She fully intended to bliss out, floating endlessly into serenity as she fought fiercely to maintain her stability, holding onto her joy.

After all, Crystal remembered, you really do not have to show up for *every fight that you are invited to…*

For this was <u>not</u> what life was truly about. Life was all about sitting under the shade of a humongous pecan tree, nibbling on a generous slice of peach cobbler pie while sipping on some refreshing ice-cold lemonade. Feeling blades of fresh-cut grass between your toes, as the sun gently caressed your bare legs. Or treading along the shoreline of your favorite beach on a hot sunny day, squishing a million grains of sand beneath your feet as you're serenaded by the soothing surf of crashing ocean waves. Like in her Malibu dreaming...

Life was not about being under attack in the urban jungle of the big city. Nor was it about flaunting your Mercedes-Benz, Louis Vuitton bag, or huge mansion high up in the hills. Life should be filled with nourishing connections. Connections with nature. Connections with a higher power. Feeling your divine spirit bond with all humanity, as you revel in time-honored family traditions, cultural heritage, and artistic creativity. Ultimately, these were the important things that mattered in one's existence. Besides, no amount of luxury vehicles, designer handbags, or prestigious living quarters could ever replace a warm hug or the sensation of truly being loved by someone special.

All decision-making requires a measure of power. Personal power. It takes some control to first make a decision, then decide to abide by the consequences that come with choosing that particular option. By choosing to forgive, Crystal was exercising her right to take back control of her emotions, and therefore, take back control of her life! She simply had to give up the grudges that held her back from truly enjoying her life.

Although she didn't really feel like forgiving all of the perceived wrongs that had taken place during her earlier years, she realized that she would be forever stuck in a rut until she dug up the *root of bitterness* that was causing a blockage in her spirit. It was slowly threatening to turn her into a fuming, cynical, scornful old woman. And she was too sexy for that to happen!

Thus, these past offenses were trying to block her future blessings. Albeit, she felt justified in her righteous rage. No one could ever take that away from her. Yet she had to move forward, in order to forgive the offenses that she diligently kept score of all these long years. On this incredible journey of self-discovery, there was no more room left for excess mental or emotional baggage. For now was her time.

In other words, before God could forgive her for her own trespasses, she had to forgive those who had trespass against her. She had to just *LET IT GO*! She had to not only let go of the anger, she had to abandon those previous burdens that sought to weigh her down.

This was her due season to reap a harvest of good tidings. This was her era to receive an abundance of riches, the likes of which she'd never known! All she had to do was give up her taste for revenge and reach out to grasp the word of God. She had to trust God to remove all hindrances and energy drainage points from her aura. After all, it was His word that was her daily nourishment. It alone held the promise of a brighter future and endless days of happiness, peace, and joy. While all her other fruitless investments came back bankrupt, this was a check that was sure to be cashed!

But what exactly did forgiveness look like? Crystal realized that for all her higher levels of education, and innate sensibilities (always trying to employ logic and reasoning in all of her decision-making processes), she didn't have a clue as to what forgiveness looked like!

Her mother had never modeled this for her. She was always quick to bring up shameful items from Crystal's past and throw it back up in her face, to remind her of her shortcomings. By consistently mentioning her daughter's relationship errors and career-related mistakes, Clarissa Turner Knight was exhibiting behavior that showed that Crystal's slip-ups would forever be held against her in the annals of time.

Seizing every opportunity to point out what someone is doing wrong- this is not how a parent displays mercy and forgiveness! No wonder Crystal had problems with being able to let go of a grudge. The *apple doesn't fall too far from the tree*, now does it?

Speaking of trees, constantly trying to please her finicky mother was like hugging a prickly cactus plant- the longer she held on, the more it was gonna hurt her!

After much deep thought and soul-searching, Crystal finally made up her mind that she wouldn't let other people's actions determine how her own character developed over time. It was definitely better to choose *movement* over *misery*. There was no reason to be stuck in a rut, when she could easily climb her way out of this pit of despair. She had to speak truth to the lies.

Forgiveness was really about deciding to possess a "generosity of spirit," and that concept would allow her heart to go from old stale energy to a fresh, reinvigorated state of being. It released her to pursue her goals and dreams, while putting her best foot forward every single day of her life. In order to offer up the finest version of herself to the world, she had to release that bitter mentality of being hateful, stingy and miserly. She would never again allow darkness to change her identity, and try to consume her very soul.

Crystal chose to expand her heart, and embrace love instead. Despite mounting frustration, she just had to take the high road. Perhaps it was time to put the past behind her to start embracing a new reality- one that involved two new notions: *acceptance and surrender.*

PART TEN

"All that is necessary for the triumph of evil
is for good men to do nothing."

Edmund Burke (1729-1797)

CHAPTER 46

Arriving home earlier than expected from a designer runway fashion show, Crystal opened the door and walked into a straight up 'mancave' gathering. The first thing she noticed was the smoky atmosphere full of the stench of finely wrapped Cuban cigars, as well as the unmistakable scent of spilled Budweiser beer. As she stood there in complete shock, the sound of dominoes being slapped down on her glass diningroom table greeted her ears. Trying to decide what to do first, Crystal just put her hand on her hip and scanned the room. It wasn't everyday that Dellevega had a bunch of rowdy male cop friends come over to their house. Was this his idea of a raunchy bachelor party?

Not finding any strippers on the premises, Crystal dropped her swag bag and walked over to give her swain a kiss on the cheek. The men stopped their card games momentarily to give her looks of approval, nodding their heads that she was, indeed, a good catch. Crystal just smiled, coughed intermittently, and waved to everyone like a reigning beauty queen at the annual Miss America pageant. It didn't faze her to be surrounded by a crowd of drunk, horny old men. She was already accustomed to this. Not to mention that she'd been with every nationality on the face of the earth in her lifetime- so she got along with *everybody.*

After being introduced to a few of the key fellas, she yawned and headed upstairs to sort through the gratis given at the wedding gown showroom. Having eaten a little too much sushi, she had a stomachache. Laying down to take a brief nap, Crystal awoke to less noise going on downstairs. Curious as to what they were up to now, she quietly crept down the steps to spy on the conversation. Listening to the uniqueness of each man's accent, she was able to identify a few of the voices. Dellevega had told her so much about his band of merry men during evening discussions after dinner.

Apparently, a dozen or so guys had already left for the night. Sitting at the bottom of the staircase, straining her ears to hear what the remainder were talking about at the table, Crystal suddenly heard them mention Juan Rosario Ortega. Imagine her surprise to discover that the dominoes game was over, and instead Dellevega and his cronies were planning an off-the-record, completely unsanctioned, covert hit on one of Ortega's major operations! She instantly wanted in on the action, but knew that as a girl, no one would take her seriously if she volunteered her services. So instead, she crouched down like a black cat and eavesdropped.

From the gist of the conversation, it appeared that Mr. Ortega was running a money laundering, guns, and cocaine conglomerate out of a six-story abandoned warehouse on East 138th street in the South Bronx. It was the perfect New York City headquarters for his empire because: 1) the loading dock had plenty of parking for his trucks; 2) the area was deserted at night; and 3) its location near the Third Avenue Bridge made shipments into Spanish Harlem and the Upper West Side a lot easier to avoid detection from police.

Still, a snitch had given up its true location, and now Dellevega's crew was devising a plan to blow the whole brick building sky high! As they described the minutiae of this one last caper, Crystal retrieved a pen and notepad from the bedroom. Jotting down the critical details, along with the projected date, she wanted to make sure she had everything written correctly. The men planned their sting operation well into the wee hours of the morning, but Crystal didn't budge. As they were finishing up with the schematics she recognized the following players in the conspiracy-

Montenegro: He was half-Australian, half-Samoan, half-Fiji and half-Tonga. That was a lot of halves, and they added up to one great big bear of a guy. He was easily the size of two regular people put together. An ex-professional wrestler who decided to join the ranks.

McGrady: An Irish lad who was led by his stern principles of good triumphing over evil. He was great with guns, a dead-on shot with aim, but only when sober. He never met a glass of whiskey he didn't like.

Percy: A corporate recruit from Trinidad, he started off working in financial investment firms as technical support. Soon he graduated to being a hacker, but found that he could have job stability with the police.

Hyde: Was that even his real name? Was he originally from Russia, Bosnia, Albania, Serbia, or Yugoslavia? No one knew for sure. He was known as a Dr. Jekyll- Mr. Hyde type of character because he spoke many languages and switched identities/ personalities often.

<u>Fu Shan</u>: A master of explosives, he learned about gunpowder, home-made fireworks, and dynamite kegs as a young boy in mainland China. Having only three fingers on his left hand, it seemed like an obsession.

Crystal waited until the multi-cultural militia left, then silently crept back up the stairs. Jumping into bed, she faked like she was snoring when Dellevega slid in next to her. She knew that he was chomping at the bit for some early morning nookie, but she'd promise to wait until they were officially married before she would let him make love to her once more. By the time they fooled around on their wedding day, it would be *FIRE!*

CHAPTER 47

On the morning in question, Crystal arose extra early. She could barely sleep the night before, so electrifying was the thought that she was going into battle tonight. Beating Dellevega to the breakfast table, she waited until he was seated, then she pulled out a small vial of holy water and starting praying in circles around him.

He was used to seeing her do weird things like marathon scrubbings of the entire house with disinfectant, then lighting many candles and saying "God bless this house, God bless this house" over and over again. Coming from a half Cuban, half Puerto Rican household, these activities were actually reminiscent of his mother and grandparents. It was a little piece of home to him. It's not that Crystal was overly superstitious, but it meant that her childhood introduction to the occult bonded them in all spiritual matters- they'd had somewhat similar upbringings.

What made this behavior odd today was the fact that he was about to embark on a very dangerous mission. Dellevega, along with five other members of his hastily assembled motley crew, were venturing into enemy territory later on tonight. Therefore he needed these blessings. He needed someone to pray for them.

Crystal spied his familiar tattered duffle bag sitting on the livingroom floor, and knew that it was full of recon equipment. He was probably going to be on this stakeout for twenty-four hours straight. She could see the sandwiches and water bottles packed up in the cooler bag on the kitchen counter. Although Dellevega had been released from the taskforce weeks ago, it was admirable that he still believed in this honorable cause.

Enough to pursue it at his own expense. After all, he had nothing but time on his hands now. No clock to punch. No dirty supervisor to placate. He had a clear head, but needed to relieve his conscience that he had done all that he could before finally calling it quits. Sometimes a man just has to do this, just has to redeem his pride by putting himself at risk. No guts, no glory!

"Going to the gym this morning, babe?" Crystal rubbed his bare shoulders and back, tracing the dragon vs. phoenix tattoo that he got inked while in the army.

"Yeah, I'm in the mood for a monster workout today. Don't wait up for me, dear, I'll be home really late."

Crystal smiled down at her lover with such benign sweetness, pecking him on the cheeks and forehead. She could've been nominated for an academy award for her acting. For they both knew darn well that Dellevega did not own a gym membership! But these were two people who were cut from the same cloth.

Two headstrong folk who didn't mean to deceive, but were so intent on achieving their dubious goals, that they wouldn't let anything or anyone, stand in the way.

Didn't they both swear to let go of this vendetta in front of Father Fulligan? Were they trying to lie to God? No, for the good Lord knows the true intentions of a man's heart, and comes swiftly to the aid of those who walk the narrow path to righteousness and justice.

In a classic *Mr. & Mrs. Smith*-type fashion, they sat and ate breakfast, producing idle talk for conversation. Crystal spoke about how she was going to start packing boxes soon for their move to the West Coast. Dellevega complained that he didn't feel like wearing a stiff tux on his wedding day. For once in his life he wanted to shuck protocol and don an outfit that felt as comfortable on him as his boyhood pajamas. Crystal thought that was a rebellious notion because she had just left a deposit on the perfect wedding dress. And so on, and so on... Neither party acknowledged that Dellevega was planning on wading into deeper waters.

Realizing that he could be seeing her for the last time, Dellevega suddenly stood up and bear hugged Crystal.

"Baby, you know that I love you, don't you? There are times that I don't get a chance to tell you just how valuable you are to me. You make life worth living!"

"I know, sweetheart. And I won't even tell you to come back to me, because I already prayed a hedge of protection around you. By the way, do you really trust these gym buddies of yours? Do they got your back?"

Dellevega gave Crystal a knowing look, forgetting that he often underestimated her woman's intuition and powers of deduction. This was not an ordinary female.

the ceiling. Walking over to a large wooden crate, she saw hundreds of handguns, pistols, and AK-47s packed in together. She was so engrossed in the discovery, she didn't hear the felon creeping up behind her. Grabbing Crystal by the throat, he had her in a strangling chokehold. Shifting gears, she stomped on his foot and elbowed him in the ribs. Then Crystal used her acrobatic training to climb a few vertical steps up onto the crate, and land herself in reverse position behind him. When he swung around to face her, out came a dagger into his heart.

Just then, the distinct sound of rapid fire machine guns drifted up from the floor below. Crystal didn't know if Dellevega was in harm's way, but she had to act fast. *Every man for himself!* Reaching into her goodie bag, Crystal retrieved her gas mask, heavy duty gloves, and the bottle of combustible battery acid. Just as she was about to launch it as far away from her as possible, she sensed movement out of the corner of her eye. Crouching down quietly, she waited until she could identify whether it was friend or foe. By the flame of a cigarette lighter she could see the faces of two men.

"Don, it's me. I'm hiding over here!" Crystal cried out.

Dellevega came limping over with Montenegro, who had been shot in the leg. Crystal quickly tended to his bullet wound with some healing ointment. Wrapping a bandana around the injury to stem the bleeding, it formed a poultice but he still needed medical attention.

"McGrady shot most of their henchmen, but someone triggered an alarm and the police will be here soon. Percy was able to hack into their computers and activate a virus that will shut down their global network of communications. Hyde has disappeared, and Fu Shan is downstairs setting the explosives. We gotta get out of this building- ASAP!" Dellevega turned to go towards the emergency exit staircase, but Crystal drew back. *"See you at home, babe."* There was one last thing she needed to do. Kissing him gently on the lips, she pushed her stunned lover away.

When Crystal was sure the two men had cleared the floor, she put on her gas mask and gloves. This joint was about to light up like a tinderbox on the Fourth of July! Too bad all that money would end up blown to bits, stoking the flames like confetti in a chimney. Hurling the bottle of toxic sulfuric acid as far away from her as possible, she pulled the pin out of a grenade and lobbed it across the room. Having packed up her bag to the max, she hauled it double-time back up to the roof to do a fantastic base jump to freedom.

Crystal was preparing to do a critical leap of faith for the second time in her life. Just as she was about to throw herself over the side of the building, praying to deploy her parachute and safely land six stories below, she turned around and beheld a strange apparition. The grenade successfully ignited the sulfuric acid, which when combined with Fu Shan's dynamite explosives, produced a blinding display of fireworks. Crystal felt the overwhelming heat scorching her face, knowing that the roof was going to cave in any second now.

But she could not take her eyes off of this heavenly vision. Out of the flames came an angel, floating on a cloud and dressed in a long flowing white robe. He assured her that the saints were proud of her efforts, all performed in faith. He also stated that like those fellow believers: Shadrach, Meshach, and Abednego, she would pass through the fiery furnace and not get burned. Lastly, he informed her that when she awoke at the next sunrise, she would realize that the war was over, and *she never had to kill again...*

CHAPTER 51

Crystal had a methodical mind and a meticulous eye for details. A perfectionist in every way, she learned to intensely scrutinize even the smallest nuances of a particular situation. By carefully examining a person's pride, preferences, and past penchant for indulgences, she could accurately predict just how a compulsive individual would react to a given set of circumstances.

It was all in how she played the game. She was determined to not only stay one step ahead of her foes and adversaries, but come out triumphant in the end. Whatever Crystal wants, Crystal gets. Those who underestimated the degree of cunning and wisdom with which she operated, usually found themselves on the receiving end of a devastating blow of crushing disappointment. For Crystal *always* came out on top!

Crystal didn't mean to be so calculating and cold-blooded. That's just the way things were in this insufferable life. She couldn't avenge every single transgression committed in the world, however, here was one wicked piece of evil that she *could* tip the scales of justice on. It was an attempt to seek Redemption, and balance out the universe in favor of what is good, right, and wholly acceptable to the Lord.

No, it wouldn't eliminate all violent acts or heinous crimes, but it would prevent the continued senseless slaughter of more innocent children. So if it required her making the ultimate sacrifice, then she was totally prepared to do that! No one needed to encourage her, or even publicly acknowledge her role as a vigilante superhero. Crystal already knew she possessed the power to procure superior results, and see to it that her honorable agenda be completely accomplished. God, nevertheless not mine, but Thy will be done on Earth.

Sangre por sangre. There is no remission of sins without the shedding of blood; yet the blood of victims speaks from the ground, and the good Lord heareth it.

That's why she simply couldn't leave well-enough alone with her campaign of revenge and retribution. Even though it was indeed a treacherous road to have traveled down, she just couldn't forget all about it. She was like a pitbull with a bone, and wasn't quite ready to let it go yet! She would make sure that Juan Rosario Ortega got exactly what was coming to him.

"Let it ride," her friends moaned whenever she spoke about her childhood trauma. They really had no idea.

"You need to shake off these shackles of bondage," her family had pleaded with her during past conversations.

"This sick obsession with Mr. Ortega must come to an end!" Dellevega insisted after his own attempt stalled.

Oh yeah, it would come to an end, alright. Eventually. Very soon. Only it would not happen how everyone thought it would. It was now game-on! Crystal was about to get things popping, fully turned-up, and all the way live! No one could predict what she was up to next. Crystal was a hot steppa, and this time when she came, she was gonna come correct. This was the end.

Ortega mistakenly thought he was untouchable, just because he was surrounded by an impenetrable wall of secrecy and submission. He assumed that he was invincible. Purely unstoppable on his rise to the top. However, no one was above the law. *NO ONE!* His loyal followers, twisted evil henchmen, and corrupted minions had been blindly obeying his demented orders for nearly three decades, yet all that was about to halt.

But was it necessary to have held onto this grudge for thirty-five long years? And why was a big-whig like Mr. Juan Rosario Ortega so hell-bent on destroying a little damsel like Dr. Crystal Knight-Davenport? Because this was no imaginary injustice: she was a first-hand eyewitness to him killing her older sister in the woods of Virginia, and murder has no statute of limitations. Now the hunter had become the hunted.

Crystal had finally found the weakest link in the chain, and it was about to be exposed. After many, many weeks of painstakingly careful planning, she'd woven an intricate web of deception and betrayal. Like a spider coming for its prey, this would be an encounter from which there was no immediate escape. This time she would not fail in her mission. This time she would gain the upper hand and righteously prevail in victory.

"You catch more flies with honey than with vinegar, dear." Crystal remembered the words her mother used to say to warn her against acting out of a spirit filled with anger and bitterness. Crystal knew, however, that revenge is a dish that's best served cold. For what goes around, comes back around. Karma always gets you in the end. Payback is a bitch, and *then you die...*

CHAPTER 52

Mr. Juan Rosario Ortega sat leisurely sipping from a porcelain cup of hot mint tea on a secluded, open-air balcony in a luxury hotel in the ancient city of Fes. Pinky finger extended outward, like the finest of 'old-money' aristocracy, he casually scanned the *New York Times* real estate section for any exciting properties. Each profitable acquisition he was able to negotiate, brought him one step closer to achieving his childhood dream: becoming the richest man in the whole world.

Hail Caesar. He was a demi-god and eventually he wanted every human being on earth to bow down to worship him. What started out as an idle fantasy, was fast turning into a true reality. He'd just finish investing a half billion dollars in an oil rig operation in Nigeria. All those years of pimping and kidnapping would be permanently behind him now. For he was finally a powerful and respectable businessman. Even the drug cartels knew better than to mess with his solid infrastructure of dedicated mules and foot soldiers.

Over the course of the last twenty years, he'd developed a reputation for consenting to swift action. His sadistic character was etched in stone, and his taste for ruthlessness was legendary. That's how he was able to maintain such loyalty. Everyone knew that he didn't just kill off his traitors, he wiped out entire families. Which was just what he was going to do when he found out who authorized the hit on his Bronx warehouse outfit. Those amateur sleuths cost him millions of dollars in lost merchandise. It was going to take weeks to get the operation back to where it was.

As he sat contemplating his next move, his thoughts were interrupted by a handsome young man who introduced himself as a concierge. Mr. Ortega had already made arrangements for an around-the-clock butler to attend to his every need, so he looked at the messenger very closely. Strange enough, he didn't look like he hailed from Morocco. Although he had smooth, tan skin indicating a Mediterranean-type background, he didn't speak with a French accent.

"Important package for Mr. Juan Rosario Ortega. This is you, no?" The envoy held forth a small present, prettily wrapped in gold metallic foil. The square box had a huge, expertly-tied bow on top, and sat on a plush scarlet red pillow. This presentation made him curious as to what contents were hidden on the inside.

Probably just your average errand-runner, I'll ask the hotel to beef up security around here, thought Ortega. He gave the young boy a scathing look, then dismissed him with the wave of a hand. Seeing that he was not going to receive a gratuity for his service, the kid retreated quickly into the adjacent dining room area.

Ortega glanced lazily at the sun setting on the horizon, noting how it turned the evening sky into the oddest shade of blood-orange. He had never before seen a crimson dusk such as this in his life, and figured that it must be just an anomaly. Or a bad omen. Turning his attention back to his surprise little gift, he tugged on the ribbon, which had a simple note inscribed on it:

For the man who has everything, here is more of what you truly deserve...

After undoing the fancy ribbon, and greedily tearing off the lavishly decorated wrapping paper, Ortega discovered that inside of the initial box was *yet another box*. Then inside of that box was a royal blue velvet pouch with a golden drawstring threaded along the top. Removing his reading glasses, Ortega rose slowly from his chair and proceeded to lean over the glass railing of the balcony to get a better look at the diminutive cargo in the dwindling light. Handling the pouch with the utmost of care, he peered closely at its contents. Pouring the miniscule items into the palm of his hand, he was mesmerized by the rich sight that brightly greeted his intense gaze. This was unexpected.

Diamonds!

Fearful to drop a single one, he gasped at the heart-stopping beauty of the icy sparkling gems. They glimmered in the soft sunlight, sending off a spectrum of scintillating brilliance. Then suddenly, just as he was standing erect, wondering which one of his faithful worshippers could've possibly sent such an expensive tribute to him, an assassin's bullet speedily ripped through his right eye socket and exited out the back of his head. The impact of the shot blasted half of his rear skull and brain matter onto the mosaic tiles of the lushly-appointed private terrace. It all happened so fast, his body was still twitching in the aftermath.

However, before his tall, slender frame could even hit the floor, another formidable Sicilian assassin silently stepped out from behind the giant stucco column to stab him viciously in the back. Feeling his long, sharp blade connect with the victim's spine, he twisted it violently, then carefully reached around to retrieve the priceless gemstones out of Ortega's clutching grip.

The diamonds had been in his family for many years before that jewelry store heist, and now the packet was finally back where it belonged. Pausing just long enough to spit on the cooling corpse of Mr. Juan Rosario Ortega, Scopetti withdrew a high-powered flashlight and small mirror from his coat pocket. The trap was set and the greedy mouse gladly took the bait.

Signaling to his partner hiding off in the distance that the target was indeed eliminated, he quickly disappeared into the shadows to avoid risking detection. Leaving just as quietly as he had appeared, Scopetti tucked away the deadly diamonds before scurrying off to meet with Cardone. Later, the two brothers compared notes as they proudly discussed their successful mission aboard a luxury yacht bound for their homeland, just off the southern tip of Italy.

EPILOGUE

On the other side of the world, Crystal was also witnessing a breathtakingly numinous moment nestling on the horizon. Listening to a non-denominational minister pronounce blessings over their sacred union, she and Dellevega stood transfixed by the mystical magnificence of this event. As she gazed lovingly into the eyes of the one and only man she had promised all eternity to, she was awed by how radically different her life was now. She never knew such joy and peace.

In the end, she could honestly forgive every single person that had ever committed a wrongdoing against her. After it was all said and done, she finally realized that nothing that they had plotted had any lasting impact on the wonderful person she eventually became. In other words, it didn't matter what anyone else said or did to try to hold her back- she was still able to keep marching on. She had no choice but to post up, because she was still destined to be fabulous!

It was as if Crystal had done a complete 180° turn from being a hot mess. *'Cause when you know better, you do better!* In such a short span of time, she lost weight, launched an exciting new career, gave up heavy drinking and decided to move to a sunshine state. Add to that, the fact that she was getting betrothed to the very special man of her dreams on a peaceful, pristine beach in wonderful Hawaii. Crystal was an overcomer who was able to make it through the thunderous rain.

Pay it forward. Maybe it was a good idea that she canceled the big wedding plans and paid off her brother's steep medical expenses instead. No one seemed concerned about where the money had come from, but oh how everything had changed for the better since then! After the pre-marital counseling session, it occurred to Crystal that this was her moment. This was her fortune; the life she'd always wanted and fantasized about. All of her hopes and aspirations had magically come true. Now she was finally free! Free from the bitter chains of fury and angst. No more burdens from the past to carry forth.

Free from decades of harboring shame, inner hatred, and debilitating self-loathing. Free finally, to explore all the good promises that this world had to offer. The cycle was complete. On this journey to mature womanhood, Crystal had finally come full-circle. She was able to sever the ignorant cord of doubt with the mighty sword of self-knowledge. Triumphing over adversity and temporary insanity for the first time in nearly thirty-five years, the future that lied ahead was actually looking rather bright for her and Dellevega.

And she did not have to sacrifice her dignity on the way to her destiny! Her past, along with all of that debilitating pain and anxiety, was all behind her now. She could finally close the book on those unfortunate events that plagued her conscience-including the savage, untimely death of her beloved older sister, Kim. Crystal understood that none of the drama from her childhood could hurt her in this present time. She could literally put all of her troubles into a small lockbox, seal the lid tight, then bury it away deep underground somewhere. Far, far away from her now.

Even the flawless diamonds that had been her dirty little secret for nearly two decades had finally been returned to their rightful owner. In her newfound wisdom and maturity, Crystal realized that what she truly craved was everlasting love- not silly material possessions! At the end of the day, Dellevega made her soul want to sing. He enticed her human spirit to want to come out and play. His undying devotion was nourishing, uplifting, and positively life-affirming.

Although no one could honestly foresee or predict exactly what tomorrow might possibly bring, Crystal had a deep-seated feeling that they would face life's unexpected challenges and overcome all obstacles…

Together.

Even their dream of opening a namesake detective agency was finally becoming a reality, and they also had a first client! Having been contracted to solve the case of the deceased heiress, they were able to leave a sizeable deposit on a great piece of property in L.A.

Crystal thought about all these aspects of her new life as she slowly marched barefoot down an aisle of pillar candles that illuminated her path to sweet matrimony. Radiantly glowing in her mermaid Ramona Keveza dress and a crown of daisies, she exchanged passionate vows with her handsome prince, against a backdrop of crashing waves and the sandy volcanic shores of her beloved Hawaii. Dellevega, who chose to stay casual in a light cotton shirt and trousers, lit up when he saw his beautiful bride for the first time. His heart filled with unbridled joy as he thanked God for his blessings.

At the conclusion of their private marriage ceremony, both Crystal and Dellevega happily released white doves into the air, quietly symbolizing all that they had both given up and left behind. Just as the beautiful birds soared high up into the sky, taking the couple's optimistic wishes for the future along on their gracefully flapping wings, Crystal felt a vibrating sensation happening deep within her dress décolleté.

Taking advantage of the distraction, she juggled her humongous flower bouquet in one hand, while digging down in her ample bosom for her cell phone. Eagerly retrieving the text message she'd been anticipating all day, a lovely sense of closure began to wash over her.

While watching his vibrant bride fiddle with her phone on their precious wedding day, Dellevega nervously kicked around beach sand with his bare feet. Finally consumed with curiosity, he reached over to kiss her on the head, concernedly asking if everything was ok.

Looking up sheepishly from the small screen, Crystal's face instantly lit up with joy, pride, relief, serenity and understanding. Uttering three short words to put her brand new husband's mind at ease, she simply said:

"Daddy, it's done!"

Thank God- it was all finally over. Or was it? For Crystal, her dark journey as a confused Knight was coming to a definitive end. However, as she prepared to step into the light of their celebrated union, she didn't realize that the true battle was only about to begin...

Topics For Discussion:

1) Do you think there was a better way for young Crystal to deal with the troublemakers that bullied her?

2) Was there a direct link between young Crystal's stay at the juvenile delinquent facility, and the mental dysfunction that she experienced later on in life?

3) Was Dellevega right for checking her cell phone?

4) Was Crystal wrong for throwing Dellevega out of the house after their heated argument?

5) Have you ever loved someone so intensely that your life seemed meaningless without that person in it?

6) Was is selfish for Hassan St. Baptiste to force his sexual desires upon Crystal, despite vowing celibacy?

7) Is it possible to follow Dr. Susanna Smith's advice: deciding to move forward, forgiving without misery?

8) Did Juan Rosario Ortega receive the fate that he deserved after committing a lifetime of sin?

9) Was there a better way for Crystal to deal with her family; would you have paid Ray's medical expenses?

10) Was there any one particular character with which you identified with the most? If so, who and why?

Greetings from lovely New York City!

Congratulations! You have successfully made it to the end of the **DEADLY DIAMONDS** trilogy of books.

We sincerely hope you enjoyed this reading experience. Remember that the journey of 1000 miles begins with a single step. Start pursuing your true life today, and leave your own legacy!

May all your tomorrows shine a little brighter…

Love,
Chyna Dixon-Kennedy

Greetings from lively Los Angeles, California!

Never stop pursuing your dreams…

May your path in life become *Crystal* clear!

A special preview of the forthcoming installment
in the Davenport & Dellevega detective series:

Crystal Clear,
Rock Star Revealed!

- - - - - - - - - - - - - - - - - - - -

Davenport and Dellevega are back to solve another mystery! This time, a wealthy heiress becomes a gruesome discovery in a park in Southern California. Their brand new detective agency is enlisted to get to the bottom of this peculiar crime; but it isn't long before they both come under attack while searching for clues.

Once they agree to investigate the death of the rich socialite, they are thrust into a whirlwind of strange happenings, unexplained vanishings, and secret societies that will stop at nothing to maintain their power. The more they uncover, the more they get sucked into a swirling vortex of lies, deception, public scrutiny and private persecution. Appearing at the center of this complex controversy is a rising rock star whose popularity is contagious, and a presidential election candidate whose true agenda remains undisclosed.

Just when Crystal thought her troubles were all over, she encounters a new series of foes that threaten to steal her newfound joy, and dismantle the paradise that she and Dellevega envisioned together. The fate of the entire nation is in jeopardy, so to even up the odds, they call upon a few old cronies to help them reveal the apocalyptic plan. Before it's too late…

About the Author

Chyna Dixon-Kennedy holds two graduate degrees, a Masters in Public Administration and a Masters in Counseling. She developed a love of writing at a very early age, compiling a collection of poems as a young girl, while nursing a penchant for mystery novels. A former fashion model, jewelry designer, and licensed cosmetologist, she has worked behind-the-scenes in the beauty industry for many years. Inspired by a passion for socio-political issues that affect women and children globally, Chyna regularly conducts seminars about overcoming obstacles in life. Her aim is to provide a voice for at-risk individuals through the use of literature. She has traveled across America and around the world extensively, and can be contacted at **cdkbooks@ gmail.com** to schedule an interview.

Printed in the United States
By Bookmasters